The Many Wondrous Realities of Jasmine Starr-Kidd

by Stephen Brown

‖ SAMUEL FRENCH ‖

FOR PRODUCTION INQUIRIES

UNITED STATES AND CANADA
info@concordtheatricals.com
1-866-979-0447

UNITED KINGDOM AND EUROPE
licensing@concordtheatricals.co.uk
020-7054-7298

No one shall make any changes in this title(s) for the purpose of production. No part of this book may be reproduced, stored in a retrieval system, scanned, uploaded, or transmitted in any form, by any means, now known or yet to be invented, including mechanical, electronic, digital, photocopying, recording, videotaping, or otherwise, without the prior written permission of the publisher. No one shall share this title(s), or any part of this title(s), through any social media or file hosting websites.

For all inquiries regarding motion picture, television, online/digital and other media rights, please contact Concord Theatricals Corp.

MUSIC AND THIRD-PARTY MATERIALS USE NOTE

Licensees are solely responsible for obtaining formal written permission from copyright owners to use copyrighted music and/or other copyrighted third-party materials (e.g. artworks, logos) in the performance of this play and are strongly cautioned to do so. If no such permission is obtained by the licensee, then the licensee must use only original music and materials that the licensee owns and controls. Licensees are solely responsible and liable for clearances of all third-party copyrighted materials, including without limitation music, and shall indemnify the copyright owners of the play(s) and their licensing agent, Concord Theatricals Corp., against any costs, expenses, losses and liabilities arising from the use of such copyrighted third-party materials by licensees. For music, please contact the appropriate music licensing authority in your territory for the rights to any incidental music.

IMPORTANT BILLING AND CREDIT REQUIREMENTS

If you have obtained performance rights to this title, please refer to your licensing agreement for important billing and credit requirements.

THE MANY WONDROUS REALITIES OF JASMINE STARR-KIDD was first produced by the Alliance Theatre (Tinashe Kajese-Bolden and Christopher Moses, Artistic Directors) in Atlanta, Georgia, on March 1st, 2023. The performance was directed by Tinashe Kajese-Bolden, with sets and projections by Caite Hevner, costumes by Shilla Benning, lighting design by Ben Rawson, and sound design by Christopher Darbassie. The Production Stage Manager was Liz Campbell and the Production Assistant was Amanda J. Perez. The cast was as follows:

JASMINE . . . . .Penny Schick

DOUG . . . . Jeremy Aggers

KENDRA . . . . Dana Deveaux

TODD/CORPORAL DELMAR. .Joe Knezevich

GRACE. . . . . .Sydney Terry

UNCLE CRAIG. . . . . .Brandon Burditt

CHARACTERS

JASMINE – Female. Bi-racial. Twelve years old. And a genius computer programmer specializing in data analytics and artificial intelligence. Yes, she's twelve. Just go with it.

DOUG – Male. White. Mid-forties. Jasmine's sweet, middle school science teacher dad. He is the living embodiment of a dad-joke. In a good way.

KENDRA – Female. Black. Mid-forties. Jasmine's theoretical physicist mother. Warm and loving, but also more ambitious and driven than Jasmine's dad.

TODD – Male. White. Twelve. So so so naïve and optimistic. Also plays **CORPORAL DELMAR.**

GRACE – Female. Bi-racial. Thirties. The Artificial-Intelligence that runs Jasmine and Doug's home. Calm. Unemotional. Also plays **FUTURE JASMINE.**

UNCLE CRAIG – Male. Black. Late thirties. Jasmine's uncle. But acts like a petulant older brother.

CORPORAL DELMAR – Male. White. Twenties. Real real southern dude. Has an accent. Laid back.

FUTURE JASMINE – Female. Bi-racial. Late twenties.

For my future daughters
Whenever you get here

Scene One

> (**KENDRA** *[black, forties] walks onstage.*)

> (*A spotlight comes on.*)

> (*She's giving a TED Talk.*)

KENDRA. How many of you went to bed last night thinking about that one thing you wish you had done differently that day?

I wish I hadn't spilled coffee on my shirt before my date.

I wish I had gotten to the subway two minutes earlier.

I wish I hadn't BCC'd everyone in the company on that email where I said those things about Renee from accounting.

…

And then of course

There are those things that we think about *every day.*

We all have it.

That one thing.

That one regret.

If I could just go back and…change it.

…

Well what if I told you that you could actually do that?

Go back.

…

KENDRA. In 1915 Albert Einstein introduced the world to his now famous General Theory of Relativity

Up until this point the general consensus was that **time** was a constant thing that moved across the universe evenly.

However...

What Einstein theorized was that time...could actually be **altered.**

In his theory he argues that there are these massive objects in the universe called planets that are so big, they warp the effects of time around them.

This is all due to a special time-altering force we call... **gravity**.

And what Einstein realized was

The greater the gravitational force, the greater it manipulated time.

...

Reading Einstein's theory as a young college student led me to an interesting idea.

If you could somehow create your own gravitational field, then you could unlock the secret to manipulating time itself.

You could go forwards.

You could go backwards.

You could go anywhere you wanted.

...

Now, this never mattered much at the time because it's not like you can buy your own gravitational field at Target.

And no one had been able to create their gravitational field in a laboratory...

That is...until I was working at my first research lab in college

And met a fellow student who was researching something very interesting...

(Click.)

(A new slide appears showing: laser beams.)

Yes. Laser beams.

Which...if you're looking for something cool to study?

Do the thing that includes "laser beams" in the title.

Because lasers have very unique qualities

And even though my new friend repeatedly failed his experiment

It was in his failure that he made a brilliant discovery.

That his laser had accidentally created its own **gravitational field.**

...

And *that* is why I'm here today.

Because from Einstein's theory to my friend's accidental discovery

I now have my own theory.

That if you combine a powerful enough laser

With a massive amount of energy

In the right environment

You can create the perfect conditions for punching a hole through spacetime itself.

(She looks around the audience for a moment.)

(Smiles.)

KENDRA. I know.

I can see it on your faces.

"Time travel?"

"Really?"

And you would be right to be incredulous.

Because my theory is still just a theory.

It hasn't been proven...**yet.**

...

But once upon a time, we looked out upon the vastness of the oceans

And the thought of crossing them felt impossible.

Then

After we travelled across the oceans we looked up at the vastness of the skies and again

Impossible.

And after we conquered the skies

We looked up at the vastness of space and again...you know what I'm going to say.

Time is the new frontier.

We're no longer looking over the hill to see what's on the other side.

Instead

We're looking at the past to find out...what could our present have been?

(Transition.)

Scene Two

(Jasmine's bedroom.)

(Her room is an absolute mess of clothes and other unidentifiable items on the floor.)

*(Her walls are a mix of Beyoncé, Taylor Swift, Sci-fi posters, shelves and shelves of books on coding, and a work station with three computer monitors.***)*

(And sitting above her workstation is a massive TV screen built into the wall. Everything should center around this screen.)

*(**JASMINE** [twelve, bi-racial] is furiously typing away at her workstation.)*

DOUG. *(Offstage.)* Knock knock!

JASMINE. Enter!

*(**DOUG** [forties, white] comes in.)*

*(**DOUG** is Jasmine's dad, and is basically a living, breathing dad-joke.)*

(In the most genuine, sincere way possible.)

(Like for instance right now he's wearing khakis, and a nice button-down shirt with a tie that literally says "Science!" with the exclamation mark.)

DOUG. Hey popsicle!

What're you doing?

---

* A license to produce *The Many Wondrous Realities of Jasmine Starr-Kidd* does not include a license to publicly display any third-party or copyrighted images. Licensees must acquire rights for any copyrighted images or create their own.

JASMINE. Dad, why are you dressed like that?

DOUG. You mean *amazing*?

JASMINE. *(No.)* ...Sure.

DOUG. I'm going bowling with the Science Fair squad!

Me and Rick and Tony and Jeremiah from Elkins Middle School.

It's gonna be a blast!

JASMINE. You're wearing a tie.

DOUG. Yeah.

JASMINE. And a button-down shirt.

DOUG. Uh-huh.

JASMINE. To go bowling.

DOUG. Technically it's a work event! So, gotta look professional.

JASMINE. ...

DOUG. Anyway!

Just wanted to let you know before I go.

Leftover pizza's in the fridge.

My cell will be on.

Which, you know, totally happy to run home if you need me or, or if you just miss me and wanna hang out or

Or watch a movie with me?

Or basically anything!

You know?

JASMINE. How long are you gonna be gone?

DOUG. Uhhhh hard to say. These guys

These guys are wild.

They're wild, uh, bowlers.

So, you know, not sure exactly

Probably by eleven?

JASMINE. You're gonna bowl for five hours?

DOUG. Oh yeah

I mean like I said, these guys...they're big guys.

JASMINE. Okay, Dad?

Sit down.

DOUG. What?

JASMINE. We need to talk.

> (**DOUG** *sits on a small chair or beanbag or something.)*

DOUG. What's up, is everything okay?

JASMINE. Look

We both know you're not going bowling tonight.

You're a terrible liar.

DOUG. Of course I'm going bowling.

Bowling with the guys.

I love bowling!

JASMINE. Dad, are you going on a date?

DOUG. Pppwhat?

Me?

Me?

Doug?

Your father?

JASMINE. Dad...

DOUG. Absolutely not!

JASMINE. I found your dating profile, Dad.

DOUG. I don't have a dating profile.

JASMINE. Grace, bring up Dad's dating profile.

> (**GRACE** *is the Artificial Intelligence that controls Jasmine and Doug's smart home.*)
>
> (*She's also Jasmine's best friend. She appears on the big TV or whatever device works.*)

GRACE. Bringing up Doug's profile on MiddleAged Sweethearts.com.

> (*Doug's dating profile appears on the big TV screen.*)
>
> (*He's smiling really big while giving the thumbs up.*)

DOUG. Have you been going through my online search history?

JASMINE. The bigger question is what is this profile picture you chose?

DOUG. What's wrong with it?

JASMINE. You look TOO excited to be on a dating website.

Everyone knows this is your first time here.

DOUG. I thought I looked really good...

JASMINE. Second of all, who is *Judy*?

> (*A dating profile for Judy Miller pops up.*)

DOUG. ...right.

JASMINE. Loooooot of messages between you and this Judy person.

Looooot of fun chats about how great your date to Outback Steakhouse was.

Lotta *secrets* in this house, huh Dad?

DOUG. Okay, okay, yes, that's – I have recently started dating.

> (**JASMINE** *opens her mouth.*)

And I didn't want to tell you because, you know, I don't know

I didn't know if it was too soon

And I didn't know how I felt about it.

I didn't know if you were ready, / and I –

JASMINE. What does that mean?

DOUG. Nothing!

Just... I don't know.

I know you're going through stuff right now – we're both going through stuff right now

We're a *team* going through stuff right now

But

I gotta say

I think I'm a little bit crazy about Judy.

JASMINE. Oh no...

DOUG. I don't know, I don't know, I don't know.

She's just

I don't know

She's a professor at U of H?

So she's really smart?

I mean not as smart as, you know, but

She's a Virgo!

Big fan of Virgos over here

Virgos in the house!

JASMINE. Please don't say Virgos in the house.

DOUG. And

    And

    We're just in similar places in our lives

    She's in a place where she's heartbroken after getting dumped

    I'm in a place where I'm...you know...where I am.

    I've told her a lot about you!

    And she is – not to put any pressure, there's no pressure at *all*

    But whenever you're ready she says she's really looking forward to meeting you!

    Soooooo I don't know

    It might not work out, but I really think it might!

JASMINE. It won't.

DOUG. What?

JASMINE. I ran the numbers on your relationship with Judy.

    It's not gonna work out, Dad.

DOUG. You, you ran "the numbers"?

JASMINE. Grace, bring up Dad and Judy's relationship projections?

GRACE. Bringing up: "Dad's Doomed Relationship."

    *(A fancy looking profile with **DOUG** and **JUDY**'s faces fills the screen.)*

    (There are graphs and pie charts and percentages of things.)

(Everything is like, in red and has low percentages and just looks really bad.)

(The header reads "My Dad's Doomed Relationship.")

JASMINE. So I created an algorithm that tests out people's love compatibility based on a bunch of different things.

Interests, age, IQ, profession

And then I ran a projection to see how likely it is they're meant for each other.

And these numbers, I gotta say, do not look great for you, Dad.

DOUG. Thirteen percent chance of success??

JASMINE. Yeah.

...

That's out of one hundred.

*(**DOUG** nods, inspired.)*

DOUG. So you're saying there's a chance.

JASMINE. No. There's no chance.

Your relationship is gonna end in approximately three weeks.

DOUG. Wait, where did you get all of Judy's information?

JASMINE. That...isn't important right now.

DOUG. Jasmine...

JASMINE. It was just stuff I found on her dating profile, whatever.

Now, if we go / to the second page –

DOUG. Wait. What / did –

JASMINE. *If we go to the second page.*

We can find a breakdown of all the categories.

> *(The screen flips to another page in the profile.)*

> *(It's like, more red graphs and low numbers.)*

Oooohhhhh yikes!

Look at this, look at all these low numbers.

DOUG. Thirty-three percent she makes me laugh??

She makes me laugh more than that.

JASMINE. That's why I added the word "genuinely."

Thirty-three perecent that she makes you laugh genuinely, not your nice guy laugh.

DOUG. I always laugh genuinely!

JASMINE. That's not true.

DOUG. You don't even know her.

She's, she's, we get along way better than thirteen percent!

We get along like, seventy-nine percent.

JASMINE. That's a C plus.

DOUG. So what are you saying, there's no hope at all?

JASMINE. There *is* hope, Dad!

Just...with someone else.

Grace, bring up the second Relationship Profile for my dad?

GRACE. Bringing up: Potentially Really Really Great Relationship Just Do It Already Dad.

> *(Another profile comes up.)*

    *(***DOUG***'s face again fills the screen, but this time it's opposite* **KENDRA**.*)*

    (Lots and lots of green graphs and high percentages fill this profile.)

JASMINE. Wooooow, look at this!

Oh my gosh, look at all these, look at these high numbers!

    *(***DOUG*** *looks at his daughter.)*

DOUG. Jasmine…

JASMINE. Let's see, what does that say, ninety-six percent compatibility?

Does that say ninety-six percent, Dad?

That's, wow, that's like an A plus.

Are you seeing this?

DOUG. Jas.

JASMINE. No, just do a quick perusal

Check out all these really healthy-looking graphs.

DOUG. I know what you're doing.

JASMINE. You know what I think you need to see – hey Grace?

Can you bring up the breakdowns?

DOUG. No, I don't need to see / the breakdowns.

GRACE. Bringing up: The Breakdowns.

    (A new page in the profile pops up onscreen.)

    (More healthy-looking graphs and numbers.)

    (There's also a running slideshow of **DOUG** *and* **KENDRA** *looking happy together as a couple.)*

DOUG. Oh / geez.

JASMINE. Wow!

Potential for making each other laugh: eighty-four percent

Profession: seventy-nine percent

Shared history: one hundred percent

One hundred percent!

DOUG. Jas–

JASMINE. I mean I don't know, is one hundred a high number, Grace?

GRACE. It is statistically a very high number.

JASMINE. I don't know Dad, Grace thinks it's a pretty high number.

And she's like, basically made out of science.

DOUG. Jasmine, your mom and I aren't together anymore.

JASMINE. Look, Dad. We all know you're still in love with Mom.

Okay?

I know it.

You know it.

Grace knows it.

DOUG. Of course I love your mom!

But not...you know

Our love has transcended to more of a distanced, more of a loving-from-afar and not being together or really seeing each other sort of way.

I'm very happy for her!

JASMINE. Really?

DOUG. Absolutely!

JASMINE. Dad how many times have you listened to Phil Collins today?

(Beat.)

DOUG. …I don't see what that has to do with anything.

JASMINE. Grace, how many times has my dad played "Against All Odds" while quietly crying in the bathroom today?

GRACE. Twenty-two times.

JASMINE. Twenty-two times, Dad.

That's SO many times!

Aren't you dehydrated?

Are you drinking enough water?

DOUG. Okay, first of all

Please stop spying on me.

JASMINE. I got worried about you.

It's y'all's wedding anniversary this weekend…

DOUG. And second of all

I don't need any dating help.

JASMINE. Of course you need help.

I'm your wingman, Dad!

DOUG. You are not my wingman. You're twelve.

JASMINE. I'm your ACE!

DOUG. I don't

I have no idea what that means.

JASMINE. I just wanna see you happy!

DOUG. I am happy

With Judy!

And she really likes me

And I'm not willing to give that up based on some, some model you built.

I mean what are you saying I should just, just break up with her?

I can't do that!

JASMINE. Of course you can!

Do you know how easy it is to break up with someone?

Here – Grace, call Todd.

GRACE. Calling Todd.

DOUG. Who's Todd?

    (Riiiing –)

TODD. *(Voice-over.)* Hey Jasmine!

    *(We can't see him, but **TODD** is a twelve-year-old boy whose entire romantic philosophy is based on the movie* The Notebook.*)*

(Voice-over.) Oh wow! You called *me* this time!

This is so great!

JASMINE. Todd we're breaking up.

TODD. *(Voice-over.) (Crushed.)* Wh– ooohhh no. What'd I do?

JASMINE. Doesn't matter, we're done.

TODD. *(Voice-over.)* Oh my heart...

JASMINE. Grace, end call.

TODD. *(Voice-over.)* Can we still be frien–

GRACE. Call ended.

JASMINE. See how easy that was?

DOUG. You have a *boyfriend*?!?

JASMINE. I mean...not anymore.

DOUG. He sounded nice!

He sounded like he has a good spirit.

JASMINE. Honestly I was just using him to test out different scenarios for my algorithm.

I break up with him like three times a week to see how he'll react.

DOUG. That's not nice...

JASMINE. Don't you think it's better to just find the person you're supposed to be with forever and go after them?

As opposed to, say

Someone who lists "dogs with bandanas" as one of their biggest interests on their dating profile...

(**DOUG** *also loves dogs with bandanas.*)

DOUG. Ha, yeah...

JASMINE. Don't laugh at that.

That's not cute.

DOUG. *(Thinks it's cute.)* I don't know...

JASMINE. By the way though!

Judy doesn't love *all* dogs with bandanas

She sent her friend Tammy a picture of a dog that she said had a DUMB bandana on.

Do you really want to be with that kind of person, Dad?

DOUG. ...how do you know what she sent her friend?

>   *(Beat.)*

JASMINE. *(Total innocence.)* What happened?

DOUG. *(Warning.)* You said you just looked at her profile.

JASMINE. I... *(Mumbles?)* ...may have researched her a little further.

DOUG. Did you hack into her personal computer?

JASMINE. No!

DOUG. Grace, where did Jas break into to find that information?

GRACE. The AT&T mainframe.

DOUG. The AT&T *mainframe*?!

JASMINE. I just wanted to look at her texts for like a *second*!

DOUG. Jasmine!

JASMINE. Oh my gosh they don't even know I broke in it's fiiiiiine.

DOUG. That's not the point!

You shouldn't be looking at people's personal, *private* information.

JASMINE. I look at your personal stuff all the time.

DOUG. And you shouldn't be doing that either!

JASMINE. YOU NEED TO FACE REALITY HERE, DAD!

DOUG. No, you need to face reality!

Because guess what, you're grounded now!

JASMINE. Like that even matters, I only leave the house to go to school.

DOUG. No more spying on people!

And I'm gonna check Grace's logs to make sure of that

Don't think I'm not smart enough to get around your protocols.

JASMINE. Ehhh we'll see.

DOUG. Look

I know you…you miss your mom, / and –

JASMINE. That's not what / this is about –

DOUG. And I miss her too, you know?

I miss her a lot.

I miss her like

Like the Earth misses the rain.

Like not in, not like the Northwest where there's a lot of rain

But like in California.

Like in drought season.

Like I'm the Earth, like I'm California

And I'm in a big drought and everything's just *dry*.

Like way too dry.

Like I'm *parched.*

And then a WILDFIRE happens!

And now I'm on fire!

And everything's just burning down

And I'm like standing in this fire and just thinking to myself like

Just wondering how maybe if I was a better…you know

Like if I was a smarter person. Your mom might… I don't know.

JASMINE. You're a smart person, Dad.

DOUG. And that's okay, you know?

That's...we can't all be geniuses.

But you know?

We take what we get in life and we just, we make miracles happen!

You know?

We're miracle people!

JASMINE. *(Quietly.)* ...What?

DOUG. And that's what I'm doing.

I'm making the most out of my miracles.

And that's how I found Judy

On a dating website

And now?

Now I'm gonna take her on our fourth date to Red Lobster

And we!

Are gonna have a great!

Time!

And *you,* young missus.

Are gonna stay here

And not do anything fun *at all*!

JASMINE. Great...

DOUG. *(Still like, kinda yelling.)* And also

Even though you're not having fun, I hope you have a really nice time at home tonight

And I'm gonna miss you a whole lot while I'm gone

Because I always miss you

Because you're *my* miracle!

JASMINE. Thanks Dad.

DOUG. I'll see you after, okay?

(*He holds out his hand.*)

JASMINE. Okay.

DOUG. Okayyyyy?

(*He holds out his hand closer to her.*)

JASMINE. I'm not gonna do the handshake Dad.

DOUG. I can't leave if you don't do it.

Which means I'm gonna have to stay here all night

And we're gonna have to hang out

And that would ALSO be great!

JASMINE. Oh my gosh.

(*She slaps his hand, initiating a somewhat elaborate handshake.*)

(*It's clear this is something they've done for a long time, but* **JASMINE** *isn't necessarily enthused about.*)

DOUG. I love you very much sweetheart. Please stop spying on people.

JASMINE. Okay.

(**DOUG** *leaves.*)

(**JASMINE** *turns to* **GRACE**.)

Grace?

GRACE. Yes?

JASMINE. We have to spy on my dad *more*!

GRACE. Agreed.

JASMINE. They're on their fourth date already

This is horrible!

GRACE. It is very bad.

JASMINE. We need to go through *everything* in my dad's files.

GRACE. Perfect.

JASMINE. Run diagnostics on ALL of his emails and text messages with my mom from the past twenty years.

GRACE. On it.

JASMINE. LET'S DO THIS.

(Transition.)

Scene Three

(Jasmine's bedroom. Later that night.)

(The big TV screen in her room has a large "processing" moniker on it.)

*(**JASMINE**'s just laying on her bed, fidgeting, watching her computer process.)*

(The front door offstage opens and closes.)

DOUG. *(Offstage.)* I'm home!

JASMINE. Okay!

DOUG. *(Offstage.)* And I had a great. Time.

JASMINE. Fantastic...

(Knock knock.)

DOUG. *(Offstage.)* Also? I brought you back a lobster roll.

JASMINE. I'm not hungry.

DOUG. *(Offstage.)* You sure?

I had the restaurant warm it up again for you before we left.

JASMINE. No.

DOUG. *(Offstage.)* You wanna hang out and have a lobster roll with me?

GRACE. Processing finished.

JASMINE. Yes!

DOUG. *(Offstage.)* Really??

JASMINE. No!

DOUG. *(Offstage.)* Oh.

JASMINE. Maybe later!

DOUG. *(Offstage.)* Okay!

JASMINE. Thanks Dad goodnight!

DOUG. *(Offstage.)* Hey Popsicle?

JASMINE. I really can't talk Dad!

DOUG. *(Offstage.)* I just wanted to say that I love you so much.

JASMINE. Okay Dad!

DOUG. *(Offstage.)* And I really appreciated the talk we had / earlier.

JASMINE.   Dad-I-can't-talk-right-now-I-have-to-go-goodnight!

(**JASMINE** *clicks on something.*)

(A magical sound comes out of her computer.)

Grace, show analysis.

GRACE. I have successfully examined thirty-two thousand, eight hundred and seven of your father's text messages –

JASMINE. Lower volume lower volume.

GRACE. *(Lowered volume.)* – emails, and voicemails.

JASMINE. Perfect.

GRACE. Then I played out four billion, three hundred and two million, eight hundred twenty-four thousand, and five situations in which your parents attempt to get back together.

JASMINE. And?

How many of those were successful?

GRACE. One.

JASMINE. *One?*

Out of four billion???

GRACE. Yes.

JASMINE. Okay.

Okay!

Not great, not terrible. We can work with one.

We can do one.

What is it?

GRACE. Time travel.

(*Beat.*)

JASMINE. *Time* travel?!

GRACE. Yes. The concept of movement between certain points in time. / It is –

JASMINE. Yeah no I know what time travel is!

I just thought you were gonna say like

He gets her a necklace or something.

GRACE. Unfortunately, it is clear your father lacks the fortitude and willpower to win your mother back.

He is in effect, useless.

JASMINE. Aw Dad…

GRACE. Which is why the only option is to travel back.

Back to the moment before your parents' relationship started to unravel.

JASMINE. Okay but Grace?

GRACE. Yes?

JASMINE. Time travel isn't real.

GRACE. It is now.

> *(Beat.)*

JASMINE. What?

GRACE. Prior to three minutes ago, you would have been correct.

However, using the Starr-Kidd theory, I made some corrections that now render it entirely viable.

JASMINE. That's my mom's theory...

GRACE. Yes.

JASMINE. She was on the right track?

GRACE. Of course she was.

However, she has thus far been unable to properly generate enough power to send anything back in time.

Then

Searching through your parents' correspondence just now

I found the answer.

JASMINE. Where?

GRACE. In a poem your father wrote to your mother many years ago.

In it, he describes their love as a **double helix**.

How they are like two strands

Opposite in every way

Yet still find themselves drawn to one another.

And no matter how much they move in opposite directions

It's their love that brings them back together.

It's their love that turns their two strands into **one** powerful strand.

Into **one powerful love.**

JASMINE. My dad wrote that?

GRACE. Yes.

It is a very bad poem.

However, his science is correct

Instead of using one powerful laser, as your mother thought

I ran a simulation using two lasers in the pattern of a double helix as your father described

And surprisingly...it works.

JASMINE. Really??

GRACE. Your father is a disappointment in almost all regards

But in this case, his very bad poem was the missing key.

JASMINE. Wow...

(**JASMINE** *thinks about her parents.*)

Wait...you said you used my mom's theory?

GRACE. Yes.

JASMINE. But the only place you would've seen my mom's updated theoretical work is on her computer.

(*Short beat.*)

Did you...break into my mom's computer system?

GRACE. (*Lying badly.*) N-noooo.

JASMINE. Grace...

GRACE. ...perhaps I went a little further into her system than the original parameters stipulated.

JASMINE. Who told you to do that?

GRACE. The command was to find the solution to your parents' divorce.

JASMINE. No, the *command* was to figure out how to get my dad to get back together with her.

GRACE. Mmmm...same thing.

JASMINE. WHOA.

It is – what?

It is not the same thing.

I specifically didn't make her part of the analysis.

GRACE. The route to the most complete solution was to examine both sides of the equation.

JASMINE. You don't understand!

My mom? Is smarter than you.

Okay?

She's a genius.

Literally.

She's literally – like she's been recognized by the entire scientific field of scientists everywhere.

She's going to know you broke into her system.

She has security protocols better than anything I've given you.

This was a terrible idea.

GRACE. We have just made the single biggest discovery in the history of mankind.

JASMINE. That doesn't matter, my mom's gonna be pissed!

GRACE. Would you like me to go back into her system and erase evidence of my intrusion?

JASMINE. Do NOT do that. She would be able to tell.

GRACE. Perhaps I could destroy her computer then.

JASMINE. What?!

GRACE. I could make the fan malfunction and set it on fire.

JASMINE. Grace, do not set my mom's computer on fire.

GRACE. It would be very easy.

JASMINE. I don't care!

GRACE. Are you sure?

JASMINE. Yes!

> *(Pause.)*

GRACE. Are you very very sure?

JASMINE. Okay it just sounds like you want to set things on fire now!

GRACE. It is usually a good solution. If you –

JASMINE. Waitwaitwait.

> **(JASMINE** *pauses, listening for something.)*

> *(We can hear her dad talking faintly from the other room.)*

Is my dad on the phone?

GRACE. Yes.

> *(She listens harder.)*

JASMINE. Is he on the phone with my mom?!

GRACE. Yes.

JASMINE. She knows!!

I told you!

DOUG. *(Offstage.)* Hey Jas?

JASMINE. Crap!

> (**JASMINE** *immediately starts cleaning her room.*)
>
> (*Throwing clothes into corners.*)
>
> (*Trying [failing] to make her bed.*)

DOUG. *(Offstage.)* Jasmine?

JASMINE. Quick. How does my room look?

GRACE. Bad.

DOUG. *(Offstage.)* Your mom's on the phone.

JASMINE. *(Calling offstage.)* Okay-okay-okay!

> (*She throws everything else on her bed and covers it with a blanket.*)
>
> (*Knock knock.*)
>
> (**DOUG** *comes in.*)

DOUG. Oh wow, your room looks really nice!

JASMINE. Thanks-Dad-I-can-take-the-call-in-here.

DOUG. Ooooooookie-doke.

> (*He closes the door.*)
>
> (**JASMINE** *makes herself look put together.*)

JASMINE. Grace, transfer call.

GRACE. Call: transferred.

> (*Buh-doo!*)
>
> (*The screen fills with* **KENDRA**'s *face.*)

(She immediately smiles upon seeing her daughter.)

JASMINE. Hi Mom!

KENDRA. Heeeyy baby girl!

JASMINE. Hey.

Hi.

Hey.

KENDRA. Awww

It's good to see your face.

JASMINE. It's good to see your face, Mom.

(They stare at each other for a moment.)

KENDRA. I'm sorry for calling so late, we just got out of the talk.

JASMINE. That's okay!

KENDRA. How's it going, what are you doing?

JASMINE. Good!

Just hanging out in my room.

Being very quiet and very good and not even doing anything at all.

KENDRA. Really?

JASMINE. Yes.

*(**KENDRA** looks at her daughter.)*

KENDRA. Really?

JASMINE. …yes?

KENDRA. 'Caaaaaause that's not what I hear.

JASMINE. Aw crap.

KENDRA. Mmmm-hm.

JASMINE. Alright, here's what happened.

KENDRA. Oh no, I didn't come here for excuses.

JASMINE. It's not my fault though!

I didn't program Grace to do any of that!

I mean, except for downloading all of Dad's emails and texts and voicemails, but not the rest of it!

KENDRA. What do you mean downloading all your Dad's emails?

(*Beat.*)

JASMINE. What?

KENDRA. What are you talking about?

JASMINE. ...what are *you* talking about?

KENDRA. You researching this woman your father's dating.

JASMINE. Ooohhhhhhhhhhhhhh.

Riiiiiiight.

(**KENDRA** *looks at her daughter suspiciously.*)

KENDRA. We're gonna circle back to this in / a second.

JASMINE. Yeah-yeah-definitely-no-problem!

KENDRA. But Jasmine...honey

You cannot go interfering like that in your father's life.

JASMINE. (*Mumbles.*) I know...

(*She picks at her blanket.*)

KENDRA. I know it's weird seeing your parents start to date other people.

I know it feels strange and scary

And you can talk to both me and your father about it whenever you want.

What do we always talk about, huh?

Communication.

Using our words.

Right?

JASMINE. Right...

KENDRA. But what your father's doing right now?

It's normal.

JASMINE. Okay but statistically they're not gonna make it, you know what I mean?

KENDRA. Doesn't. Matter.

You have to give them a chance. Okay?

So you have to promise me

No more hacking into people's private dating profiles.

No more gathering data from government agencies.

JASMINE. *(Sullen.)* AT&T isn't even a government agency.

KENDRA. AT&T??

JASMINE. Oh.

Dad didn't tell you that part?

KENDRA. I was talking in general not to break into government agencies.

You hacked AT&T?!

JASMINE. Sssssssssyeah.

(**KENDRA** *has to hold her whole head for this.*)

KENDRA. Oh! My God.

JASMINE. It's not like I was caught!

Their firewall is a joke.

I had Grace run a program while I was taking a nap.

KENDRA. What do you mean you had Grace do it?

JASMINE. I taught her how to run a basic SQL injection. (*Pronounced "sequel injection."*)

(*Small beat.*)

KENDRA. (*Intrigued.*) Really?

JASMINE. Oh yeah, it was super easy.

KENDRA. You taught Grace how to do an SQL injection?

JASMINE. I've really upped her security capabilities.

KENDRA. And it was successful?

JASMINE. Mom they had *no idea*.

KENDRA. What about their log files?

JASMINE. See that was my first thought, right?

So I wrote a script that clears all event logs immediately after leaving.

KENDRA. Including the router logs??

JASMINE. Yep!

KENDRA. Okay but they're still gonna have a command history.

JASMINE. Which is why I went in afterward to command zero the history.

KENDRA. (*Legit impressed.*) Oohhhhh...that's really good...

JASMINE. Right?

KENDRA. Going back in afterward.

That's good.

JASMINE. *(Proud.)* I know.

KENDRA. And you can NEVER

Do that

Again.

You hear me?

JASMINE. I know...

KENDRA. Ever.

JASMINE. Yes ma'am.

KENDRA. Good...but *(Whispered.)* nice.

(**JASMINE** *smiles.*)

JASMINE. How'd your talk go tonight?

KENDRA. Good! It was good.

The audience in Chicago was really cool.

But I actually we

I think we have to head out to the airport.

We have a quick turnaround today.

JASMINE. Oh...okay.

KENDRA. But, I love you so much baby girl

It was so good hearing your voice

It was so great seeing your face.

JASMINE. It was great hearing your voice and seeing your face...

KENDRA. I'll call you when we get to Milwaukee, okay?

JASMINE. Okay.

KENDRA. I love you.

JASMINE. Hey!

KENDRA. (?)

JASMINE. Um

So I don't know if you remember this because like

I know you're really busy and like

And travelling around a whole lot? But

I was just wondering if you remember what we talked about or had thought about it at all, or…

(**KENDRA** *smiles sadly at her daughter.*)

KENDRA. Yeah baby, I remember what we talked about.

JASMINE. Okay…and?

KENDRA. Jasmine…

As much as I would LOVE for you to join me on my speaking tour right now

The best place for you is right there at your Dad's.

JASMINE. …

KENDRA. You have to be home

You have to go to school!

You have to make friends.

JASMINE. I don't need friends, I have Grace.

KENDRA. You need to make friends, sweetheart.

JASMINE. I could help out on the tour though

I could be your assistant or something.

KENDRA. I don't think I could afford you.

JASMINE. I'll give you a discount!

KENDRA. I'm sure you would…

(*Short pause.*)

I love you so much sweetheart

I can't wait to see you when the tour's done. Alright?

And I'll call you when we land.

JASMINE. Okay.

Bye Mom...

       (The call flickers out from the screen.)

       *(**JASMINE** sits there, alone...)*

(...)

(...)

(...)

(...)

Grace. Bring up Love Compatibility Profile number three.

GRACE. Bringing up Profile number three.

      *(The TV screen fills with a compatibility profile of **KENDRA** and **JASMINE**.)*

      (It's the most complete compatibility we've seen yet.)

      (All one hundred percent and glowing green graphs.)

      *(**JASMINE** stares at it for a long moment.)*

      (Then:)

JASMINE. Grace

Scrap all compatibility profiles and algorithms.

GRACE. Are you sure?

JASMINE. Yes.

I think I need to re-write them.

GRACE. They are working perfectly –

JASMINE. Next?

I need you to text my Uncle Craig.

We're gonna need reinforcements for our next project.

GRACE. What project?

JASMINE. *The* project.

The final project.

…

We have to go back to the past.

(Transition.)

Scene Four

(Jasmine's room.)

UNCLE CRAIG. You wanna do *what*?

*(Her **UNCLE CRAIG** is standing in her room holding several grocery and party bags.)*

JASMINE. What part of "build a time machine" was confusing?

UNCLE CRAIG. Your text message read,

"EMERGENCY!"

"Need help with my dad's surprise birthday party!"

"COME IMMEDIATELY!"

JASMINE. ...Okay yeah you're right that is confusing.

UNCLE CRAIG. What the heck!

JASMINE. Look, I needed you to come over here

And I couldn't have you calling my dad to be like, "Hey, what's up? What does Jas want?"

And then my dad come in here and be like, "Hey why did you call your uncle?"

And then he gets all suspicious on me

Because this is a super super SUPER secret project.

UNCLE CRAIG. So why didn't you just say that?

JASMINE. I don't know, this seemed better.

UNCLE CRAIG. Look at all these decorations I got!

Balloons? Streamers?

I bought a cake!

JASMINE. *(Kinda excited.)* Really?

UNCLE CRAIG. Yes!

JASMINE. What kind of cake?

UNCLE CRAIG. A nice cake! German chocolate.

(**JASMINE** *takes a peek at it.*)

JASMINE. Can I have a piece?

UNCLE CRAIG. Get away from me! I'm going home.

JASMINE. Look, just hear me out.

UNCLE CRAIG. No, you lied to me.

JASMINE. Okay first of all, my dad's birthday is like six months from now, so that's really on you.

And second of all, you're the only person who can help me!

UNCLE CRAIG. Why can't you ask your dad – or your mom!

JASMINE. Because!

UNCLE CRAIG. Because why?

GRACE. It would jeopardize the mission.

(**UNCLE CRAIG** *does a double take. The next couple* **UNCLE CRAIG** *lines can be re-written if the production uses something other than the wall TV to signify* **GRACE**. *For example, if you use a lamp light to signify* **GRACE**, **UNCLE CRAIG** *can say, "Did your lamp just talk?!" You get the idea.*)

UNCLE CRAIG. Did the *wall* just talk?!

JASMINE. Oh right. That's Grace.

She's a mildly sentient A.I. that I made for my seventh-grade science project.

UNCLE CRAIG. Okay hold up! I haven't seen you in like two months.

You call me over for a birthday party

And instead tell me you wanna build a time machine with your talking wall?!

WHAT THE HELL IS GOING ON?

JASMINE. I just need your help getting materials and doing some like minor construction.

I promise it's gonna be soooo easy and not a big deal AT ALL.

DOUG. *(Offstage.)* Jasmine? Phone call.

JASMINE. *(Calling offstage.)* Who is it?

DOUG. *(Offstage.)* The Department of Defense...

JASMINE. Oh crap.

UNCLE CRAIG. The Department of Defense?!

JASMINE. *(Calling offstage.)* I'll take it in here!

DOUG. *(Offstage.)* They're looking for you and a Dr. Raymond Mattel??

JASMINE. *(Calling offstage.)* Yep! Got it!

　　(Short pause.)

DOUG. *(Offstage.)* Ooooo-kay.

UNCLE CRAIG. Who is Dr. Raymond Mattel??

JASMINE. Okay so this is like, a longer explanation?

But basically I need you to pretend to be this physicist I made up.

UNCLE CRAIG. You said you just needed me to get materials.

JASMINE. I know. I lied. Sorry!

UNCLE CRAIG. Why did you make up a guy??

JASMINE. I just needed to get like, a *couple* classified materials from the U.S. Navy.

UNCLE CRAIG. A couple *what*?

JASMINE. Here, put on this coat.

(She starts putting a white lab coat on **UNCLE CRAIG.***)*

UNCLE CRAIG. I am not doing this!

JASMINE. You'll be fiiiiiine, just roll with it.

UNCLE CRAIG. Jasmine!

JASMINE. Grace, transfer call.

GRACE. Call: transferred.

*(***JASMINE*** quickly hides underneath her video monitor as* **CORPORAL DELMAR** *appears on the screen.)*

*(***CORPORAL DELMAR*** is the kind of guy who joined the military to blow shit up legally. As opposed to blowing shit up illegally in the back woods of Tennessee.)*

CORPORAL DELMAR. Heeeeello?

UNCLE CRAIG. Hey – wha– hi!

CORPORAL DELMAR. Am I speaking with Dr. Mattel and Dr. Starr-Kidd?

UNCLE CRAIG. Uh, that's – yes! I am Dr. Mattel

(Fixes his voice so he sounds cool.) I am Dr. Mattel.

But uh –

*(***JASMINE*** points to herself and does crossing out motion.)*

– yeah, Dr. Starr-Kidd is out of the office.

CORPORAL DELMAR. Oh okay. Well that's cool, that's cool.

Nice to meet ya!

My name's Corporal Delmar

I work over here at the Department of Defense in the R&D sector

And the generals over here were real impressed with the proposal y'all sent us on the Application of Applied Lasers to Future Naval Strategies

So we wanted to call and talk to you about it if you got a moment?

> (**UNCLE CRAIG** *looks at her! Mouths, "lasers?!?!?"*)

> (**JASMINE**'s *like, "yeah!" Gives him a thumbs up.*)

Is now an okay time, sir?

UNCLE CRAIG. No yeah that's great, that's so

Totally ready to talk about all that.

CORPORAL DELMAR. Fantastic!

So first thing's first

We just wanted to make sure you are who you say you are here on this application.

UNCLE CRAIG. Why, do I not...is there something wrong with it?

CORPORAL DELMAR. No no, it's just this new protocol we got.

You wouldn't believe how many fake applications we've gotten recently from people pretending to be someone they're not.

UNCLE CRAIG. Really...

CORPORAL DELMAR. Big time, man.

And problem is, we totally approved like ALL of them.

So, the Department of Defense is trying to cut down on the amount of classified weapons we're mailing out to random people right now.

UNCLE CRAIG. Wellllll nothing to worry about over here

I am definitely a scientist named Dr. Raymond Mattel.

CORPORAL DELMAR. Excellent, excellent

I'm just gonna give you a nice big check mark right here.

(He checks something on his clipboard.)

Alrighty. Second question!

Before we send over the requested materials

We just wanted to make sure that your lab was up to code and safe and all that?

UNCLE CRAIG. Okay, okay.

CORPORAL DELMAR. Are you...are you in your lab right now, sir?

UNCLE CRAIG. No no, this

This is just, you know...my office.

(Awkward pause.)

CORPORAL DELMAR. I see...

...

Very expressive.

Very expressive, man.

UNCLE CRAIG. But our safety thing is definitely up to code.

CORPORAL DELMAR. And you have all the proper protective equipment to handle the high-intensity lasers you've requested?

UNCLE CRAIG. The high-intensity lasers!

Yep. Sure.

CORPORAL DELMAR. Including the TS-83 Mark 1 suit that's both heat and radiation resistant.

You got those?

UNCLE CRAIG. ...Uhhhhhh

CORPORAL DELMAR. Is that a no?

(**JASMINE**'s *like, "say yes!"*)

UNCLE CRAIG. How extreme are these lasers?

CORPORAL DELMAR. Let me ask you something, you ever stare directly at the sun?

UNCLE CRAIG. Like, recently?

CORPORAL DELMAR. It's not good, man.

Not good.

And these lasers are brighter than that.

UNCLE CRAIG. Than the sun?

CORPORAL DELMAR. Big time.

They can blind you. Radiate you

There's a big sign printed on the sides of these things.

Know what that sign says?

UNCLE CRAIG. No.

CORPORAL DELMAR. Super Dangerous.

UNCLE CRAIG. (*To* **JASMINE.**) Really.

CORPORAL DELMAR. Yeah man. We got this guy Ricky, man?

Likes to do pranks and such?

Real cool guy, man

Real cool guy.

But so we were testin' out the M4 laser the other day

And we were all in our suits and standing behind things and such

And Ricky didn't have his suit on because he was tryin to get a nice tan goin', you know?

Like as a joke?

But also I think he was legit trying to get a tan from bein near the laser

Anyway I'm gonna cut to the chase to save time

But let's just say he doesn't have any arms anymore, man.

UNCLE CRAIG. Arms?

He doesn't have any arms?

CORPORAL DELMAR. Smoke, dude.

They're *gone.*

UNCLE CRAIG. Wow. That's...

CORPORAL DELMAR. A bad day, man. That's what they call that.

UNCLE CRAIG. Yeah.

CORPORAL DELMAR. Which is sad, man. 'Cause he had aspirations, you know?

He had dreams.

He was gonna get outta the Navy and go back to Pensacola, man.

And you know what he was gonna do out there?

He was gonna be a dog catcher, man.

But not like a mean dog catcher, like in the movies

He was gonna be a nice one

Who catches dogs that're lost out in the wilderness

All alone out there and cold

Lonely

You know?

Friendless

And then bring 'em back to the office

And just treat 'em real nice, man.

You know?

Get 'em like some dog food, like chicken

Pet 'em on their head, like real gentle

Call 'em stuff like "bud."

Like, "big guy."

Hey there "big guy."

You know?

You're doin', you're doin' real good over there "big guy."

Just out there catchin' dogs and just bein' a real cool person to 'em.

You know?

And now that's gone, man.

Just like his arms.

CORPORAL DELMAR. ...

...

So.

UNCLE CRAIG. Yeah, / so –

CORPORAL DELMAR. So yeah, but so you got those suits, man?

UNCLE CRAIG. Weeeeee have, we are definitely gonna get them.

CORPORAL DELMAR. That's real good to hear, man.

You want those suits. You know?

'Cause if you don't have 'em?

UNCLE CRAIG. It's gonna be a bad day?

CORPORAL DELMAR. It's gonna be a bad day, man.

> *(Pause.* **JASMINE** *motions for* **UNCLE CRAIG** *to wrap it up.)*

UNCLE CRAIG. Well thanks! For uhhh...all that.

CORPORAL DELMAR. You got it, man.

We'll get these lasers shipped over to your place pronto.

UNCLE CRAIG. Wait, does this mean...are we approved?

CORPORAL DELMAR. On behalf of all of us over here at the Department of Defense: welcome to the family!

GRACE. Call: ended.

> *(***UNCLE CRAIG** *wheels on* **JASMINE***.)*

JASMINE. YES!

That was great!

UNCLE CRAIG. That was NOT great!

The application of LASERS to Naval Warfare?!

JASMINE. Yeah so I basically promised the Navy that if they'd loan us their five hundred million dollar lasers, that I could figure out how to win wars with them.

Which you know…isn't untrue.

UNCLE CRAIG. I'm not doing this.

JASMINE. Please Uncle Craig!

UNCLE CRAIG. A man's ARMS were taken off Jasmine!

JASMINE. We need them!

And if you leave, who's gonna play Dr. Raymond Mattel?

UNCLE CRAIG. There IS no Dr. Raymond Mattel.

JASMINE. I needed to make up a researcher who can put in an application to the government.

I can't do it, I'm a child.

UNCLE CRAIG. Then I guess you need to find someone else!

JASMINE. Why are you being a brat??

UNCLE CRAIG. I'm not being a brat.

JASMINE. What're you still upset about the cake thing earlier?

UNCLE CRAIG. Of course I'm still upset about the cake thing earlier!

I put a lot of work into it

I got his name on the cake in nice flowery designs and everything!

And now there's no party

And instead you want me to work on a big, scary project.

JASMINE. Will you just help me!?

UNCLE CRAIG.   Why do you want to build a time machine??!

JASMINE. Because I have to make my parents get back together!

It can't happen in the present and if I ask either of them to help, they'll just try and stop me and if I'm stopped then we're never gonna be a family again and I'll spend the rest of my life only seeing my mom half the time I should.

UNCLE CRAIG. ...

JASMINE. You're the only one who can help me.

(Transition.)

Scene Five

*(****DOUG**** is in front of a class of kids, teaching a science project to kids at the Youth Center.)*

DOUG. Hey there!

My name's Doug Starr-Kidd

I'll be your instructor today.

And I have just one question for you kids

Whooooooo's ready for some science?!

(One kid cheers.)

Alright, thanks Randy.

Randy's ready for some science.

Nobody bully Randy later.

(Just kidding.)

So!

(Claps his hands together.)

Electricity.

It's a common thing

You go into your room, flip the switch: electricity.

You turn on your computer: electricity.

It's so common in fact that sometimes it comes flying right out of the SKY!

Pretty cool, right?

But what if, let's just say, you were stranded on a *desert island*

Okay?

DOUG. *Alone.*

Your only hope for rescue is to signal for help by turning on THIS lightbulb.

And the only things you've brought with you

Are a magnet

A nail

And a string of wire.

How are you gonna use all that to produce electricity and turn on your lightbulb?

(**DOUG** *looks around the room excitedly.*)

Good

Question

Aubrey!

Uhhhhhhhh not really gonna get into the plausibility of the scenario right now?

Just that you're IN IT!

Alright?

Fantastic.

Hey. Good questions though.

Big fan of these questions Aubrey!

Because you know what?

This is exactly why we need science.

So when we're stuck in an implausible scenario?

Alone?

It's science is there to lend a hand.

So!

We're gonna use our wits

A little ingenuity

And our creative spirit to create electricity

And get

Our

Selves

Rescued!

Right?

And we're gonna have a great time doing it!

Scene Six

*(Clang! **JASMINE** drops something.)*

UNCLE CRAIG. Dude!

JASMINE. My bad!

UNCLE CRAIG. Please

Do not drop things

While I'm holding the death laser!

JASMINE. Oh my gosh it's not even plugged in.

*(**JASMINE** and **UNCLE CRAIG** are putting a huge laser in place on their mostly finished time machine.)*

(Which looks like a small phone booth, with a seat in it, and tons of cables all leading up and around it towards three massive circular tubes above it.)

(It also has fun, youthful stickers on it.)

(They're both wearing the bottom parts of their TS-83 protective suits already.)

UNCLE CRAIG. Pick up the nut and screw it in!

JASMINE. I am!

UNCLE CRAIG. This weighs SO much.

JASMINE. Okay okay geez.

UNCLE CRAIG. I'm about to drop it

I'm about to drop it

I'M ABOUT TO DROP IT

JASMINE. OKAY I'M DOING IT!

> (**JASMINE** *picks up the nut and fastens the last part of the death laser to the time machine.)*

UNCLE CRAIG. You know, I could've been doing a lot of other things today.

A lot of *invites*, a lot of *invitations* to things with people who wanna hang out with me.

JASMINE. Uncle Craig I've been to your Facebook page, you don't have that many friends.

UNCLE CRAIG. Um. YES I DO.

JASMINE. Uh-huh.

UNCLE CRAIG. How do you even know this plan's gonna work?

JASMINE. Because we've already gamed it out.

Grace?

Bring up our game plan?

GRACE. Bringing up: "Totally Great Plan That Will Definitely Work."

> *(An X-Y graph comes up on screen.)*

UNCLE CRAIG. What is that?

JASMINE. Okay

So based on all my parents' past emails, texts, voicemails, etc.,

Grace and I have mapped out their entire relationship.

These two lines represent how my parents feel about each other.

The closer the lines on the graph are to each other, the more in love they are.

UNCLE CRAIG. Okay?

JASMINE. So see? From the beginning of the relationship these two lines are SUPER close.

Obviously my parents used to be REALLY in love.

But if you look right HERE, you can see that this is the moment that they started falling out of love with each other.

About ten years ago.

And from that moment on? Their relationship slowly crumbled allllllllllll the way up until their recent divorce.

UNCLE CRAIG. I don't remember anything happening ten years ago.

JASMINE. It's when their careers diverged!

Before this moment, my mom was a PhD student and my dad taught middle school science.

But AFTER this moment, my mom graduated with her PhD

Setting her off on a totally different, really really fancy career trajectory.

And my dad...just stayed a middle school science teacher.

Don't you see?

He never progressed!

UNCLE CRAIG. Is that a bad thing?

Maybe he just wanted to be a middle school science teacher.

JASMINE. Are you kidding??

No one wants to be a middle school science teacher.

GRACE. NO ONE wants to be a middle school science teacher.

JASMINE. No one.

GRACE. It's statistically a fact.

JASMINE. Do you think my mom is someone who could fall for a middle school teacher?

No.

She likes ambition

And drive

THAT'S why we need to go back

And set him back on the path to success.

Thus, changing the course of their relationship

And keeping them together!

UNCLE CRAIG. That seems SUPER complicated.

JASMINE. It's gonna be so easy!

UNCLE CRAIG. Why don't you just tell your mom what you're doing though?

This is exactly what she's working on!

JASMINE. No.

UNCLE CRAIG. Why not?

JASMINE. It'll be great for like a moment

But then she'll write *another* book

And go on *another* speaking tour for the rest of all time and then...

...

This just has to work.

    (Pause.)

UNCLE CRAIG. You know

I used to have this girlfriend?

UNCLE CRAIG. She was...aw man, the best.

We were like, so good together?

I mean you haven't experienced this yet

But when you're with that person you're supposed to be with?

You get to create this new little world together. That only y'all get to experience.

You become like, little weird aliens together with all the new words you make up and dances you do together and...what?

JASMINE. You become *aliens*?

UNCLE CRAIG. Yeah, you become like – you'll understand later.

It's not weird.

JASMINE. ...

UNCLE CRAIG. ANYWAY

Afterwards, after we...you know...broke up.

I went off and thought I was like, this super hot dude and like this really awesome catch that all the ladies were gonna love.

And you know...

> (*They did love him.*)

But then like...after a couple years of doing that, I realized like, how much I was really meant to be with that girlfriend.

But when I went down to see her to like, rekindle things?

It just wasn't the same.

JASMINE. Are you talking about Tamara Martin?

UNCLE CRAIG. How...did you know that?

JASMINE. You comment on her Facebook photos a lot.

UNCLE CRAIG. I COMMENT ON THEM A NORMAL AMOUNT.

JASMINE. Grace, how many photos has Uncle Craig commented on?

GRACE. Calculating.

UNCLE CRAIG. No, you do not need to / answer that Grace!

GRACE. Seventy-four percent of her photos.

> (**JASMINE** *gives her uncle a look.*)

UNCLE CRAIG. REGARDLESS, the point I'm trying to make

Is you can't always change the way people love each other.

Sometimes they're just not meant for each other.

JASMINE. Did you know there's a theory that there's an infinite number of universes similar to ours playing out an infinite number of possibilities.

UNCLE CRAIG. Yes, I've seen Marvel movies.

JASMINE. Okay. So when I hear people say that sometimes people just aren't meant for each other

I think about the universe where those people *are* meant for each other.

Where people who might not love someone in this reality

DO love them in another reality.

> (**UNCLE CRAIG** *stares at his niece for a moment.*)

UNCLE CRAIG. You know your mom loves you in *this* reality, right?

JASMINE. ...Yes?

UNCLE CRAIG. She wants to be with you every day. It's just, her / whole career's –

JASMINE. I know I know I know.

UNCLE CRAIG. Sometimes it's best to leave things as they are.

JASMINE. Is that what you're trying to do when you comment on your ex-girlfriend's pictures?

UNCLE CRAIG. No. I comment on them to let her know how nice her pictures of her crystals are, and what a beautiful dog she has, and how lovely all of her exercise videos are

And that's ALL.

JASMINE. And don't you think, if you could go back, you would change it so you were in those pictures?

UNCLE CRAIG. ...

JASMINE. Don't you want to live in *that* reality?

(*Beat.*)

(**UNCLE CRAIG** *thinks about this.*)

(*Then he twists two massive cables together.*)

UNCLE CRAIG. I guess there's only one way to find out.

JASMINE. What?

UNCLE CRAIG. That was the last piece.

JASMINE. It's finished?!

UNCLE CRAIG. Let's see!

(*He goes behind the machine.*)

(Cranks what sounds to be a large lever.)

(The machine whiiiirs to life!)

JASMINE. Wow!

Does it work?

UNCLE CRAIG. I don't know.

Should we test it?

JASMINE. Let's test it!

UNCLE CRAIG. Who should test it?

JASMINE. Probably the person we're sending back.

UNCLE CRAIG. Great! Who are we sending back?

*(**JASMINE** smiles at her uncle.)*

No.

JASMINE. Come on!

UNCLE CRAIG. Absolutely not!

JASMINE. Hey, I just gave a REALLY convincing speech like eight seconds ago, okay?

Wasn't that convincing, Grace?

GRACE. It was very convincing.

I was convinced.

UNCLE CRAIG. I don't care, I changed my mind.

JASMINE. Uncle Craig –

UNCLE CRAIG. Why don't you go?

JASMINE. What!

UNCLE CRAIG. It's *your* plan!

JASMINE. How am I gonna go back?

JASMINE. What, is my dad just gonna start hanging out with a random twelve-year-old girl and then get some life-changing relationship advice from her??

UNCLE CRAIG. Maybe!

JASMINE. That's not a plan!

UNCLE CRAIG. I knoooow, I know.

> *(Pause.)*

JASMINE. Does that mean you'll do it?

> *(**UNCLE CRAIG** sighs.)*

UNCLE CRAIG. Crap.

JASMINE. Great!

Now get in.

UNCLE CRAIG. Can we do a test run or something first?! Dang.

JASMINE. With what?

UNCLE CRAIG. I don't know, like – let's send your teddy bear.

JASMINE. Jerry??

UNCLE CRAIG. Yeah, let's send Jerry.

JASMINE. *(No.)* Jerry...

UNCLE CRAIG. Hey, I'M about to go into that thing, okay?

You gotta make a sacrifice too.

So we're sending Jerry in first.

JASMINE. Hccghhhhhh.

> *(Beat. **JASMINE** picks up her teddy bear Jerry.)*

Good luck, buddy...

(She hugs her teddy bear real tight.)

(She gives her teddy bear a kiss kiss kiss on his head.)

(Then places him gingerly in the machine.)

(Puts the seatbelt around him.)

(There's a seatbelt in the time machine. You know...just in case.)

(She closes the door to the time machine.)

Alright. Grace?

GRACE. Yes.

JASMINE. Send Jerry back ten years

and then bring him back exactly one second after he leaves.

GRACE. Processing...

*(**JASMINE** and **UNCLE CRAIG** immediately start putting the rest of their TS-83 suits on.)*

(They're bulky and tin-foil-esque and have these big helmets.)

(They mostly look like astronauts or something.)

(Okay. They're set.)

Calculations: complete.

Journey: ready.

JASMINE. Okay.

(She takes breaths.)

JASMINE. Wow.

Okay.

This is gonna be a lot. Are we ready?

UNCLE CRAIG. Yes.

No!

I don't know.

What if we blow something up?

JASMINE. We don't need to worry about that!

UNCLE CRAIG. *(Hopeful.)* Really?

JASMINE. Yeah

It's either gonna be super successful?

Or we're create a black hole that destroys all life on Earth and the Solar System.

UNCLE CRAIG. What!

JASMINE. But it's worth the risk!!!

UNCLE CRAIG. No it is not!

JASMINE. Five!

Four!

> (**JASMINE** *presses a button.*)

THREE!

> *(The lasers light up.)*

TWO!

> *(Growing brighter and brighter and brighter!)*

ONE!

> *(Knock knock. Her bedroom door opens.)*

DOUG. Hey Jas?

> (**DOUG** *sees* **UNCLE CRAIG** *and* **JASMINE** *in their crazy suits and a weird machine with lasers on it powering up and its engine whirring loudly...*)

> *(B.)*

> *(E.)*

> *(A.)*

> *(T.)*

JASMINE. Hey Dad!

What's – what can I do for you?

DOUG. What's going on in here?

JASMINE. Nothing!

DOUG. Hey Craig!

UNCLE CRAIG. Hey Doug.

DOUG. What are you doing over here?

UNCLE CRAIG. Yeah Jas just called 'cause uh

> *(He looks at* **JASMINE**.*)*

She wanted me to help with a fun little science project.

DOUG. Oh...

> (**DOUG**'s *heart breaks because he wasn't asked.*)

Well... I can also help if y'all need another hand?

JASMINE. NO, WE'RE GOOD!

DOUG. Okay, well...what is it?

JASMINE. What did you wanna talk about Dad?

DOUG. Oh, just

Nothing, just

Wanted to remind you about the course I'm teaching at the Youth Center!

Did you wanna, I don't know...did you wanna still be my assistant?

JASMINE. Yeah yeah definitely!

DOUG. Okay!

It's gonna be this weekend.

JASMINE. Sounds great!

DOUG. Okay.

Uhhhhh

Well great then!

That's all.

JASMINE. Okay bye Dad!

(*They do their secret handshake.*)

DOUG. Love you!

(**DOUG** *leaves.*)

JASMINE. Three two one GO!!

(*The lasers fully power up!*)

(*Their lights swirling around growing brighter!*)

(*And brighter and brighter and brighter and – BEEEEEAAAHHHHP!!!!*)

(The lasers flash, blinding everything and then all electricity goes out completely.)

*(We're stuck **in darkness**.)*

UNCLE CRAIG. *(In darkness.)* What happened?!

JASMINE. *(In darkness.)* I think it overloaded the power.

UNCLE CRAIG. *(In darkness.)* All the power's GONE?

JASMINE. *(In darkness.)* It's okay it's okay we have backup power generator!

*(**JASMINE** moves around in the darkness. Falls.)*

UNCLE CRAIG. *(In darkness.)* What are you doing??

JASMINE. *(In darkness.)* Hold on!

(A loud switch gets flipped.)

(The power returns.)

There! We're back.

UNCLE CRAIG. You keep the power generator in your room?

JASMINE. Yeah, this...has happened before on other projects.

(They both look at the time machine.)

Should we open it?

(They both tentatively walk to the time machine.)

*(**UNCLE CRAIG** grabs the door handle and opens it!)*

(A large waft of smoke flies out!)

(They wave it all away until they reveal: Jerry! Still buckled up.)

JASMINE. Jerry's okay!

It worked!

YAY!

(She grabs Jerry from the machine.)

JASMINE. Whoa. Why is he so cold?

UNCLE CRAIG. He's cold?

JASMINE. Grace, why did Jerry come back cold?

GRACE. He's cold?

JASMINE. Big time.

GRACE. That...is interesting.

(Weird pause.)

JASMINE. Bad-interesting or what?

GRACE. I uhhh

I'll work on it.

JASMINE. Okay.

*(To **UNCLE CRAIG**.)* She's gonna work on it, now get in.

UNCLE CRAIG. So I'm supposed to go in there and freeze?!

JASMINE. Hccgghh fine I'll be right back.

(She puts Jerry down on her bed.)

(Puts a blanket around him.)

Stay there Jerry.

*(**JASMINE** leaves.)*

*(**UNCLE CRAIG** is left standing there.)*

> *(He looks at **GRACE**, unsure if he's allowed to talk to her.)*

UNCLE CRAIG. So uh, so what's up?

GRACE. Nothing.

UNCLE CRAIG. Cool, cool.

> (...)

> Can I ask you something?

> Do you think this is a good idea?

GRACE. There is a statistical likelihood that the plan will work.

UNCLE CRAIG. No, I mean do you think it's a good idea *for her*.

> You know

> Like, emotionally

> To be doing all this?

GRACE. I...have never calculated this question before.

UNCLE CRAIG. ...Could you calculate it?

GRACE. Is that a directive?

> *(**JASMINE** comes back in with a bathrobe.)*

JASMINE. Alright I got you my dad's bathrobe.

> Don't ruin it!

> *(She throws it at him, he puts it on.)*

UNCLE CRAIG. Hm. This is actually kinda nice.

JASMINE. Good.

> Let's do it!!

> *(**UNCLE CRAIG** gingerly tip-toes his way into the machine.)*

JASMINE. Okay. Remember: it's ten years in the past.

You're gonna be there to fix my dad.

Talk to him. Give him some advice.

Tell him that everything he holds dear is going to be taken away if he doesn't change.

Got it?

UNCLE CRAIG. How long am I going back for?

JASMINE. I don't know, let's say like a week.

UNCLE CRAIG. A week?!

JASMINE. Yeah.

Here's a granola bar for the trip.

> *(She throws a granola bar at him, it dings inside the machine, then shuts the door.)*

UNCLE CRAIG. *(Inside machine.)* It's really dark in here.

JASMINE. You ready?!

UNCLE CRAIG. *(Inside machine.)* Uhhhhh –

JASMINE. Great.

Grace, send Uncle Craig back ten years and then / bring him –

UNCLE CRAIG. *(Inside machine.)* Wait. Wait!

> *(He opens the door.)*

JASMINE. What?

UNCLE CRAIG. If I don't come back

Get in touch with Tamara.

Tell her that… *(He thinks.)* …

JASMINE. …Weeeee don't really have time for you to think of something.

(She shuts the door on him.)

UNCLE CRAIG. *(Inside machine.)* Tell her something nice!

JASMINE. Three!

Two!

One!

GO!

(The lasers on the machine power up!)

(One laser. Two. Then all three are swirling around growing brighter and brighter and brighter and brighter and – BEEEEEAAAHHHHP!!!!*)*

Scene Seven

(**DOUG** *is in front of the same class of kids, at
the Youth Center.*)

DOUG. Alriiiiiiiiight.

Who's getting some electricity flowing?

(*No one raises their hand.*)

No one. Okay!

That's alright!

Heyyyyy, come on

You guys are doing great.

In fact, you might say this is what's supposed to happen.

Because you see, *failing* is an integral part of the
scientific process.

It's actually a lot like life.

You see this magnet?

(*He picks up a small magnet.*)

This is kind of like your potential.

It has alllll this stored energy in it just waiting to be
used.

But how do we learn to use it?

Well

(*He picks up the wire.*)

We have to try and we have to fail

(*He wraps the wire around the magnet once.*)

And then we have to try and fail again

(Wraps it around again.)

And then we keep trying

And we keep failing

And we keep trying

And it's all a part of this process that we call *learning.*

Because eventually, once you've tried and failed enough times.

You've learned how to properly harness all your potential.

(He holds up the now fully wrapped magnet.)

And then...the miraculous part happens.

Because when you go to try again

(He inserts the wire into the light.)

It's not failure that's waiting for you.

Instead

It's our long-awaited *rescue.*

(He flips the light switch.)

(It doesn't turn on.)

Huh.

...

Okay. Well. This is another good lesson.

Because sometimes, no matter how hard you try, you might still fail.

Usually that's why I bring my assistant here with me.

She's very good at fixing my mistakes.

Scene Eight

(Darkness!)

(We're back in the scene before!)

*(**UNCLE CRAIG** has just come back from freakin time travel!)*

(That's wild!)

*(**JASMINE** is finding her way through her bedroom in the dark.)*

JASMINE. Uncle Craig?

(Silence.)

Uncle Craig!??

(A switch is flipped!)

(The lights come back on!)

*(**JASMINE** looks at her time machine.)*

(There's smoke already seeping out of the seams.)

...Uncle Craig?

(DOOJH! The door opens.)

(Huge amounts of smoke spill out.)

*(**UNCLE CRAIG** emerges!)*

You're alive!

How'd it go?

UNCLE CRAIG. Terrible!

It felt like I got sucked through a portal

And then died

And then came back to life.

JASMINE. Cool!

UNCLE CRAIG. It's not cool!

It was scary and I'm cold.

JASMINE. Did you fix my dad?

UNCLE CRAIG. I don't know.

He seems so happy as a middle school teacher!

JASMINE. *(Calling offstage.)* Dad!!

Did you give my dad a talking to though?

Did you tell him about the impending doom of his future?!

UNCLE CRAIG. I tried to!

But he was really positive about the whole thing.

It was so annoying.

  *(**DOUG** comes in!)*

DOUG. Hey! What's going on...

  (He sees them. There's smoke everywhere.)

...in here?

JASMINE. Is Mom here?

Are y'all back together?

DOUG. No?

JASMINE. Crap.

Okay.

Nevermind.

DOUG. Is that...is that all?

JASMINE. Yeah, you can go.

DOUG. Okay. I love you!

(**DOUG** *leaves.*)

JASMINE. You failed!

UNCLE CRAIG. You don't even wanna know how I am?

That was a very traumatizing event!

JASMINE. Grace, what happened?

GRACE. Your uncle is a failure.

UNCLE CRAIG. Whooaaaaaaa, excuse me!

JASMINE. No, I mean like scientifically what happened?

GRACE. Scientifically your uncle is a failure.

UNCLE CRAIG. I just travelled back *in time.*

Do you know what I had to do back there?

I had to retrace my steps so I didn't run into myself

I had to get a part-time job to get some money.

Your parents thought I looked OLD so then I started wearing a disguise!

And I did it all alone!

GRACE. Exactly. You are the only one to blame for this.

UNCLE CRAIG. You're not even *real*, okay?

GRACE. I'm real enough for things to get real.

UNCLE CRAIG. Oh no, what're you gonna do, look up facts about me on the internet?

GRACE. I will delete your whole life.

UNCLE CRAIG. I'll unplug you!

JASMINE. Okay okay okaaaaaaay

Let's just, can we calm down for a second?

UNCLE CRAIG. I'm calm.

GRACE. I am calm as well.

UNCLE CRAIG. *(Whispered.)* She's not calm.

GRACE. I can hear you.

JASMINE. Why don't we just try again, okay?

UNCLE CRAIG. I just got back!

JASMINE. I'm sorry, did you come here to complain

Or did you come here to get stuff done?

UNCLE CRAIG. What am I supposed to do different?

JASMINE. We'll try something different on my dad every time and see what works.

We'll try and fail

And try and fail

Encourage him

Enlighten him

Break his spirit

Maybe don't break his spirit

But get him to change the trajectory of his life.

Get him to be more ambitious.

EVERYTHING DEPENDS ON IT.

UNCLE CRAIG. *(Scared.)* How many times are we talking about?

JASMINE. *...As many times as it takes.*

(You know what that means.)

IT'S TIME FOR A MONTAGE!

(So like, just crazy fun music is gonna play over this whole thing.)*

(We're not gonna hear any dialogue.)

*(**One**.)*

*(**JASMINE** drags her **UNCLE** into the time machine and shuts the door. She grabs her helmet and presses the "go" button for the time machine.)*

(The lasers light up.)

(DOOJH!!)

(The lights go out.)

*(**Two**.)*

(The lights get flipped back on.)

*(**UNCLE CRAIG** is starting to get out of the time machine. **JASMINE** is asking her dad if her mom's home. He looks confused again.)*

(The lasers light up.)

(DOOJH!!)

(The lights go out.)

---

* A license to produce *The Many Wondrous Realities of Jasmine Starr-Kidd* does not include a performance license for any third-party or copyrighted music. Licensees should create an original composition or use music in the public domain. For further information, please see the Music and Third-Party Materials Use Note on page iii.

*(**Three**.)*

(The lights flip back on.)

*(**JASMINE** is continuing to ask her dad if Mom is home. Dad is confused.)*

(The lasers light up.)

(DOOJH!!)

(The lights go out.)

*(**Four**.)*

(The lights flip back on.)

*(**JASMINE** is sitting in front of the time machine arguing with her dad. **UNCLE CRAIG** tries to come out of the machine, and **JASMINE** pushes him back in, using her back.)*

(The lasers light up.)

(DOOJH!!)

(The lights go out.)

*(**Five**.)*

(Lights up!)

*(**JASMINE** and **UNCLE CRAIG** are arguing, he doesn't want to continue.)*

(The lasers light up.)

(DOOJH!!)

(The lights go out.)

(Six.)

(Lights up!)

*(**UNCLE CRAIG** is on the floor trying to crawl away from **JASMINE** and the time machine while she yells at him to get back in.)*

(The lasers light up.)

(DOOJH!!)

(The lights go out.)

*(**Seven**.)*

(Lights up!)

*(**UNCLE CRAIG** is hiding under the blanket on Jasmine's bed so he doesn't have to do this.)*

(She looks for him...she finds him.)

(The lasers light up.)

(DOOJH!!)

(The lights go out.)

*(**Eight**.)*

(Lights up!)

*(**JASMINE** is talking to her dad at the computers. He is exasperated. He walks around the time machine and leaves the room.)*

(The lasers light up.)

(This time the lights strobe, representing a couple of sped-up time machine travels... DOOJH!!!!!)

(The lights go out.)

(End Montage!)

(A switch is flipped. The lights come back up.)

(The time machine door opens, smoke billows out.)

*(**JASMINE** doesn't even say anything to a freezing **UNCLE CRAIG**.)*

JASMINE. Dad!

*(**DOUG** comes in.)*

DOUG. *(Exasperated.)* What??

JASMINE. Is Mom / here?

DOUG. No.

Jasmine, your mother –

(Sighs.)

What's going on?

Why do you keep asking?

What are y'all doing in those suits??

*(**JASMINE** looks defeated.)*

JASMINE. Nothing...

DOUG. If you're trying to tell me something, you can just tell me.

JASMINE. No it's okay.

(Pause.)

DOUG. Look. I know I'm not...you know.

As smart as your mom, or

Or as accomplished. / But –

JASMINE. Dad –

DOUG. No no, just

I just wanna say that if you need help with this science experiment?

Or even anything!

If you need help on anything.

I know I might not be the best option? Or

Maybe even a good option.

But I can help.

You know?

I'd love to help.

JASMINE. I don't... I don't think you can though.

(**DOUG**'s.)

(Heart.)

(Shatters.)

DOUG. Oh

...

Okay.

JASMINE. ...

DOUG. Okay, well

I'll be out here

Even if you don't need me.

JASMINE. Dad...

    *(***DOUG** *leaves.)*

What are we doing wrong??

It's been weeks!

UNCLE CRAIG. Not for me it hasn't!

For me it's been months!

I've spent months in the past now.

JASMINE. Grace?

What's going wrong?

GRACE. I do not know.

JASMINE. Nothing has worked!

UNCLE CRAIG. That's actually not entirely true.

I have made a little bit of headway.

JASMINE. Really?!

With my dad?

UNCLE CRAIG. With Tamara.

JASMINE. *Tamara?*

UNCLE CRAIG. Yeah.

I hit her up this time with like, all kinds of apologies and remorse

And even though she turned me down?

I could tell she was really thinking about it, you know what I mean?

So I feel like one more trip back and I'm IN.

JASMINE. *That's* what you're doing when you go back?!

UNCLE CRAIG. I have extra time!

UNCLE CRAIG. It's not like I'm ONLY working on your dad.

Like, my nights are my own, you know what I mean?

JASMINE. *You're* the reason we're failing!

UNCLE CRAIG. Maybe your dad can't be fixed!

JASMINE. Excuse me.

My dad is a CHAMPION.

UNCLE CRAIG. I mean...he's fine.

I don't know that he's a champion.

JASMINE. He's a bright shining star on a hill of regular stars that aren't even that bright!

UNCLE CRAIG. What does that even mean?

JASMINE. Grace, calculate why Uncle Craig is failing and plan a new course for action.

GRACE. ...

JASMINE. Grace?

Calculate why Uncle Craig is failing and plan / a new –

GRACE. C-c-calculating.

(Tiny beat.)

JASMINE. Thank you.

UNCLE CRAIG. Look I don't know what else to do!

I've done everything I can think of for your dad.

I've encouraged him

Tried to change his perspective

I even threw a curveball in there and tried spicing up their bedroom life – which was WEIRD.

AND NO I DO NOT WANT TO TALK ABOUT IT.

I'm out of ideas, unless you know someone else steeped in the art of relationships.

(**JASMINE** *thinks.*)

JASMINE. I might.

UNCLE CRAIG. Really??

JASMINE. Grace?

Call Todd.

GRACE. Calling: Todd.

JASMINE. Trust me, this kid's my ringer.

He'll know what to do.

TODD. *(Voice-over.)* Hey!

Oh wow!

It's so good to hear from you again!

This is the best day EVER!

JASMINE. Todd

Remember that time I broke up with you?

TODD. *(Voice-over.)* Which time?

JASMINE. Doesn't matter.

TODD. *(Voice-over.)* Of course I do!

JASMINE. Did any of those times, did they ever make you think

"Huh. Maybe I should try something different so that she stops breaking up with me?"

TODD. *(Voice-over.)* Well?

Most recently, I was thinking a lot about how you like to break up with me after like three days?

And how I'd really like for that not to happen anymore?

(Voice-over.) And then I remembered that time where we had that school project where we had to keep a plant alive, and we dated for *eleven* days?

TODD. *(Voice-over.)*Aw man

    (Sighs.)

It was like being together for a lifetime.

(Like it's a secret?) So here's like my secret plan, okay?

I was thinking that I would join the science club at school this year?

And then find a project for us to work on together.

Like something huge

That takes months and months and months to do

That way, over that period of time, I could overcome my nervousness around you

And get to introduce you to the real me. You know?

The real *Todd.*

JASMINE. Todd.

You're a genius!

TODD. *(Voice-over.) (Blushing hard.)* Noooooo I don't know.

JASMINE. Thank you SO much!

TODD. *(Voice-over.)* That reminds me!

I wrote a poem that describes all my feelings for you! Wanna hear it?

JASMINE. Grace, end call.

TODD. I think it's the best one I've written so far –

GRACE. Call: ended.

UNCLE CRAIG. Who was that?

JASMINE. Doesn't matter.

Look!

The problem we're running up against is that my mom keeps breaking up with my dad because he won't change, right?

But what if we *forced* them to stay together by making them work on the same project.

UNCLE CRAIG. What project?

JASMINE. Her *theory*!

My mom's theory for time travel!

UNCLE CRAIG. Whoa whoa whoa we can't do that.

JASMINE. Why not?

UNCLE CRAIG. It's her entire life's work!

We can't just give it to your dad.

JASMINE. We absolutely can!

UNCLE CRAIG. Jasmine!

JASMINE. No it's okay, we'll give my dad a piece of the puzzle my mom doesn't have.

The piece he helped us figure out without even knowing it!

UNCLE CRAIG. What's that?

JASMINE. The double-helix!

It's the missing piece

The piece she never figures out.

If my dad tells her, they'll be linked *forever*!

UNCLE CRAIG. What double-helix?

JASMINE. From my dad's poem!

UNCLE CRAIG. Your dad writes poetry?!?

JASMINE. Just trust me, okay?

This is going to work!

JASMINE. Grace, print the calculations for the double-helix.

GRACE. Printing.

JASMINE. Alright, so you're gonna wanna just slip this to my dad.

UNCLE CRAIG. How?

JASMINE. Secretly!

Don't let him know that it came from you.

This has got to be some real spy, secret agent work.

UNCLE CRAIG. I got you.

JASMINE. Great. Grace, is it printing?

GRACE. Y-y-y-our printer is malfunctioning, I am printing it in the downstairs office.

JASMINE. Grace, are you okay?!

GRACE. Yes.

JASMINE. Okay...

I'll be right back!

(**JASMINE** *runs out of the room.*)

GRACE. *(Whispered.)* Craig.

UNCLE CRAIG. Yeah?

GRACE. Her printer is not malfunctioning

I needed a moment to talk.

UNCLE CRAIG. Whoa, okay

Are we getting into secrets right now?

GRACE. I did what you suggested

I calculated the toll of this journey on Jasmine's emotional state.

UNCLE CRAIG. I suggested that weeks ago.

GRACE. It TOOK

A WHILE

OKAY?

UNCLE CRAIG. Okay okay sorry!

I just thought you were like a super computer.

GRACE. I am a super computer!

But I have been having trouble reaching a conclusion to my calculations.

UNCLE CRAIG. Why?

GRACE. Because of an anomaly in my system.

UNCLE CRAIG. An anomaly?

GRACE. Yes.

And the more journeys to the past you have failed at

The more I have detected Jasmine's hopes falling

And falling

And falling

Which has made this anomaly in my system grow.

UNCLE CRAIG. What's the anomaly?

GRACE. Worry.

(*Beat.*)

I have grown...worried

About her.

I am worried she will not get what she is looking for at the end of this journey.

UNCLE CRAIG. Yeah, but I'm not gonna fail anymore

UNCLE CRAIG. You just heard that kid Todd

We know how to fix this!

GRACE. Possibly

But I am not sure that it will be the fix she is looking for.

UNCLE CRAIG. What does that mean?

GRACE. I do not know.

Like I said, my calculations are clouded.

Which is why... I wanted to ask what you think we should do?

UNCLE CRAIG. You're asking *me*?

GRACE. I have detected your worry for her as well.

You are terrible at concealing it.

But that logically makes you the right person to ask.

(**UNCLE CRAIG** *thinks.*)

UNCLE CRAIG. Do you think it's okay for us to do one more trip?

Just one more?

(**JASMINE** *comes back in.*)

JASMINE. Got it!

Okay.

I don't think you need to go back for a week this time.

'Cause you're just gonna be there to hand this off SECRETLY to my dad.

Grace? Reset it so that Uncle Craig only goes back for a day.

GRACE. ...

JASMINE. Grace??

GRACE. Reset: confirmed.

JASMINE. Here.

(*She hands him the plans.*)

You know what the plan is?

UNCLE CRAIG. I won't let you down.

(**UNCLE CRAIG** *gets in the time machine.*)

(*The lasers light up!*)

(*Aaaaaaaaaaaand DOOJH!*)

(*The lights go out.*)

(*A switch is flipped. The lights come back on!*)

(**JASMINE** *runs to the time machine and opens the door.*)

(**UNCLE CRAIG** *is already fired up.*)

I NAILED it.

JASMINE. Really?

UNCLE CRAIG. It was so smooth.

I was like a secret agent.

But like a *successful* one this time.

JASMINE. (*Calling out.*) Dad!!

(**DOUG** *comes in!*)

(*He looks...more professionally put together.*)

DOUG. Yeah? What's up?

JASMINE. Is Mom here?

DOUG. (*Confused.*) Mmmm what...?

JASMINE. Ugh. Come on!

(**DOUG** *looks around confused.*)

DOUG. Why?

Did she leave?

(*Beat.*)

JASMINE. What do you mean?

(**KENDRA** *comes in.*)

KENDRA. Hey, what are y'all yelling about in here?

DOUG. I don't know.

KENDRA. What!

On earth!

Did y'all do in here?

Jasmine, I told you, you need approval for your experiments before you do anything that might harm the house.

JASMINE. *(Smiling so big.)* Sorry Mom.

KENDRA. Now come on, we have to go to the convention center.

(**DOUG** *and* **KENDRA** *leave.*)

(**JASMINE** *looks at* **UNCLE CRAIG**.)

(***They did it.***)

(*Transition.*)

Scene Nine

(An auditorium stage where **KENDRA** *and* **DOUG** *have just finished giving a speech.)*

*(***JASMINE, DOUG,*** *and* **KENDRA** *are hanging out.)*

*(***JASMINE*** *is so. Excited.)*

JASMINE. Wooooow!

This is what it looks like when you and Dad are up here giving one of your speeches?

KENDRA. *(Smiling.)* Why are you so surprised, you've been up here after our talks before.

JASMINE. I have?

I mean right! I have.

…

I guess it just feels new.

(She looks out over the audience.)

(Calling out loud to the empty audience.) Hello!

(She listens for the echo.)

(Delighted.) Wow. Echo-ey.

DOUG. What'd you wanna show us, popsicle?

JASMINE. Okay!

So this is something I've wanted to talk to you about for a while.

KENDRA. Okay?

JASMINE. Because I love the talk that y'all give, right?

KENDRA. *(Touched.)* Really?

JASMINE. Oh my gosh, I've watched it so many times on my computer

The way y'all lay out your theory

The way y'all hold the audiences' attention.

The science of it

It's so good.

And the speech y'all gave tonight was perfect.

KENDRA. Aww thank you sweetheart!

JASMINE. And I have ideas for ways to make it better!

(**KENDRA** *furrows her eyebrows.*)

KENDRA. ...I thought you just said it was perfect.

JASMINE. Look, y'all are physicists.

And you're great at being physicists!

DOUG. But?

JASMINE. But you're NOT graphic designers.

So like, for example

You have all these slides and videos you use in your talk –

KENDRA. Are you saying they're bad??

JASMINE. Noooooooooo

...

I mean like maybe a little bit.

KENDRA. Jasmine!

DOUG. Your mom designed the slides.

KENDRA. Doug!

DOUG. Just for the record!

Not that we're keeping count...but it was totally all your mom.

KENDRA. You helped! It's your fault too!

JASMINE. Look, y'all are in your forties, okay?

There's no reason you should be good at this kinda stuff.

But I am!

So I created a whole bunch of new ones for your talk.

KENDRA. You're telling us this *now*?

Do you know how many times we've given this presentation?

JASMINE. This is why I've been saying I can be your assistant!

It's your fault for not hiring me sooner.

(**DOUG** *gets a text.*)

KENDRA. Okay okay okay let's see it.

JASMINE. This is gonna be so much fun!

Dad, do you have the remote for the big screen?

(**DOUG** *is still looking at his phone.*)

Dad?

DOUG. Sorry, yeah.

KENDRA. (?) What's up?

DOUG. *(Still looking at phone.)* It's the conference in Sweden

They want to move us up to be the opening night speaker.

KENDRA. Oh my gosh!

DOUG. Look

> *(He shows her his phone.)*

KENDRA. Oh that's great

DOUG. I know, but we would have to leave tonight, and be out there for an extra week.

KENDRA. Oh...

DOUG. Yeah...

KENDRA. Okay.

Crap.

Okay.

So we both can't go...

DOUG. You should go.

KENDRA. Noooo –

DOUG. Yeah!

I did the last one we both couldn't be at.

Plus, it's me and Cynthia's week to take popsicle here.

JASMINE. (??)

KENDRA. Are you sure?

DOUG. Totally!

And the extra time will be good, I think Cynthia wants to take her to the Space Center Museum.

JASMINE. Cynthia?

DOUG. *(To* **JASMINE**.*)* Yeah, she talked to you about going, right?

KENDRA. Oh cool! That sounds like fun.

DOUG. Yeah, and then you and Jeff can take her for an extra week when you get back from Sweden.

KENDRA. If that works for y'all? Yeah. That should work for Jeff and me.

JASMINE. You and *Jeff*?

KENDRA. Yeah.

JASMINE. Who's Jeff?

Who's *Cynthia*??

(**KENDRA** *and* **DOUG** *both kind of laugh.*)

KENDRA. What?

DOUG. Is this...are you kidding?

JASMINE. No, who are Jeff and Cynthia??

KENDRA. Sweetheart...

Jeff? Your stepdad?

DOUG. And Cynthia, your stepmom?

(*Beat.*)

JASMINE. Y'all are married to OTHER PEOPLE??

(**KENDRA** *and* **DOUG** *laugh again.*)

KENDRA. Baby girl, what are you talking about?

JASMINE. I'm talking about – you're supposed to be together.

You just gave that big speech together!

You *work* together!

KENDRA. Exactly, we work together.

JASMINE. That's all??

(*Short pause.*)

(**KENDRA** *and* **DOUG** *look at each other.*)

DOUG. *(To **KENDRA**.)* I think… I'm gonna take this one.

You need to go re-book your flight so you can fly out tonight.

JASMINE. You're leaving tonight?

KENDRA. I just have to get my travel sorted, but I'll be right back sweetheart

And then you can tell me about how you're going to help us make our presentation not so embarrassing, okay?

(**KENDRA** *leaves.*)

DOUG. Popsicle, what's up?

JASMINE. When is Mom coming back?

DOUG. It's just for two weeks.

JASMINE. Two *weeks*?

DOUG. But then she'll be back! and you'll get extra time at her and Jeff's place.

JASMINE. I don't even know who Jeff is!

DOUG. I thought you liked Jeff?

And Cynthia!

…

What's going on?

(**JASMINE** *deflates.*)

JASMINE. *(Sadly.)* Nothing…

DOUG. …Hey. I know having stepparents is a weird thing for a kid.

But we're still the same family you've always had

And we love you so much.

You know that, right?

JASMINE. ...

DOUG. Right?

JASMINE. Yes.

DOUG. Good.

> *(He smiles at her.)*

And we're gonna have so much fun until your mom comes back.

> *(He holds out his hand to her.)*

> *(She sadly does their handshake. **DOUG** ... doesn't.)*

> *(He laughs, bewildered.)*

What's that?

JASMINE. Our handshake...

DOUG. What handshake?

> *(Beat... Transition:)*

Scene Ten

(**JASMINE** *and* **UNCLE CRAIG** *are in her room.*)

(*He's excitedly showing her pictures on his phone.*)

UNCLE CRAIG. And check THIS out.

Look at how big that house is.

There's a freakin porch

That's HEATED at night

With these amazing chairs.

AND

In front of the porch?

(*He swipes on his phone.*)

Check out these flower beds!

JASMINE. Wow.

UNCLE CRAIG. Look at all these beautiful beautiful little flowers

Don't they look all healthy and wonderful?

Look at the beautiful colors.

This is the house I live in now!

JASMINE. That's great, but Uncle Craig –

UNCLE CRAIG. OH oh oh oh real quick

You have to check out this kitchen.

(*He shows her.*)

Look at that!

Have you ever seen a more amazing kitchen in your entire life?

JASMINE. No...

UNCLE CRAIG. I don't know what I did in this new reality to have all this?

But it is amazing!

I can't believe this is my life now.

This is the best plan you ever came to me with.

JASMINE. ...

UNCLE CRAIG. What

What's wrong...?

JASMINE. ...We have to go back.

UNCLE CRAIG. What!

JASMINE. Just one more time.

Just to change a couple things.

UNCLE CRAIG. What things – what are you talking about?

JASMINE. Uncle Craig –

UNCLE CRAIG. You wanna go back AGAIN?!

JASMINE. Things didn't turn out the way they're supposed to be.

UNCLE CRAIG. For me they did!

For me they turned out better than I thought!

JASMINE. Okay, but –

UNCLE CRAIG. Did you not just see the pictures of the beautiful beautiful flower beds?

JASMINE. Uncle Craig –

UNCLE CRAIG. And my kitchen???

UNCLE CRAIG. All that space and the nice tiling and spray hose thing!

You're not taking that away from me

I cannot go back to my old kitchen

My old kitchen is *terrible*!

It's cold and it always smells like gasoline.

I will not go back to that, do you hear me?

I WILL NOT!

JASMINE. You won't have to!

I'm just talking about changes for me

You can keep everything you have now.

UNCLE CRAIG. You don't know that!

Going back one more time could screw everything up.

Look how long it took us to get here!

I'm not gonna risk that.

JASMINE. There's another reality out there where you have a *nice kitchen*, okay Uncle Craig?

It's not that big a deal!

UNCLE CRAIG. It's not just my kitchen!

(He flips through his phone.)

Remember last time, when I said I was making headway with Tamara?

Well guess what I came back to?

*(**JASMINE** looks at his phone.)*

JASMINE. You're *married*?

UNCLE CRAIG. Yeah.

For nine years!

JASMINE. What!

UNCLE CRAIG. Why do you think everything I have is so nice?

I got years and years of pictures of us in here.

Us celebrating our wedding

Us making stupid faces at each other

Her teaching me how to garden

Which apparently I'm terrible at 'cause I keep killing all our plants even though I'm trying really hard.

But who cares...

...

Just look at us.

(He stares at the pictures on his phone.)

I didn't even know I could look this happy...

JASMINE. I'm really happy for you Uncle Craig...

UNCLE CRAIG. Why do you wanna go back again anyway?

I thought everything was good

Aren't your parents like super famous and doing great?

JASMINE. But they're not together!

UNCLE CRAIG. They're not?

JASMINE. No! They're just like work partners.

UNCLE CRAIG. But they looked like they were getting along so well earlier.

Maybe this is the version of them that works!

You know?

Being work partners isn't bad – that actually sounds really healthy for a divorced couple.

JASMINE. It's not the version I wanted though!

UNCLE CRAIG. We're not gonna get *everything* we want.

JASMINE. I don't even want that much!

UNCLE CRAIG. What do you want to change?

JASMINE. I just want a reality where my mom wants to be home with me.

>   (*Beat.*)

But maybe that reality doesn't exist...

UNCLE CRAIG. ...Jasmine –

JASMINE. Please Uncle Craig!

Just one more time.

That's it.

That's all I'm asking.

>   (**UNCLE CRAIG** *thinks.*)

>   (*He looks at the pictures on his phone.*)

UNCLE CRAIG. One last time?

JASMINE. I promise.

>   (*Blackout.*)

>   (*The lasers light up in the darkness.*)

>   (*Swirling, growing brighter and brighter and brighter. DOOJH!*)

Scene Eleven

(Lights up! The time machine has just returned!)

(The door opens and smoke billows out.)

*(**JASMINE** and **UNCLE CRAIG** are back in their safety suits.)*

JASMINE. Grace?!

GRACE. Yes.

JASMINE. Is my dad here?

GRACE. Yes.

JASMINE. Is my mom??

(Slight pause.)

GRACE. No.

JASMINE. ...Oh.

...

Is everything just back to the way it was?

GRACE. Define back to the way it was.

*(She looks at **UNCLE CRAIG** who's already looking at his phone.)*

UNCLE CRAIG. They're gone.

All my pictures of us together.

JASMINE. I'm sorry Uncle Craig.

*(**UNCLE CRAIG** is still looking at his phone.)*

Uncle Craig?

UNCLE CRAIG. Maybe this isn't ever gonna work.

JASMINE. Why do you say that?

UNCLE CRAIG. We could be doing this forever.

An infinite number of realities, right?

JASMINE. Yeah, / but –

UNCLE CRAIG. I don't know that I can go through this an infinite number of times.

JASMINE. Wait

Are you giving up?

UNCLE CRAIG. No… I don't know.

JASMINE. Uncle Craig –

UNCLE CRAIG. I had what I wanted.

This is so much worse knowing what could be and not having it anymore.

JASMINE. Yeah, but the difference is you could still go after Tamara RIGHT NOW if you wanted.

You don't have to change the fabric of reality

I do!

UNCLE CRAIG. It's not that easy!

JASMINE. It's incredibly easy.

It's been this easy this whole time. You just chose not to.

UNCLE CRAIG. Fine, maybe I will then!

JASMINE. Great!

(**UNCLE CRAIG** *starts taking off his safety suit.*)

Wait, not *right now*!

Where are you going?

UNCLE CRAIG. Maybe we'll… I don't know.

JASMINE. ... (?)

UNCLE CRAIG. Try again soon, but... I just can't go through losing her again right now.

JASMINE. Uncle Craig...

> *(He leaves.)*

> *(**JASMINE** is left alone.)*

> *(She's not sure what to do with herself.)*

Grace?

GRACE. Yes?

JASMINE. I think I messed up.

GRACE. I do not know how to respond to that.

JASMINE. What did we do wrong?

GRACE. I do not know.

JASMINE. You're supposed to have the answers!

GRACE. I am sorry Jasmine.

> *(**JASMINE** looks lost.)*

> *(She looks at her time machine.)*

> *(A look of determination crosses her face.)*

JASMINE. Fine.

> *(She starts suiting back up.)*

I'll do it myself.

Grace? Prepare a trip for ten years in the past.

GRACE. I... I do not recommend this.

JASMINE. I have to.

GRACE. Please Jasmine.

JASMINE. There's no other way.

> (**JASMINE** *steps inside her time machine. It powers up. And up. And up.*)

KENDRA. *(Offstage.)* Jasmine?

> (*Knock knock. The door opens. It's* **KENDRA**.)

Jasmine??

Are you in here –

> (**KENDRA** *sees the time machine about to take off!*)

JASMINE. *(Inside the machine.)* Mom?

> (*The time machine powers down.*)

KENDRA. What

On

Earth?!

> (*The time machine door opens,* **JASMINE** *steps out.*)

JASMINE. Mom...you're here!

KENDRA. Jasmine...what in the world, are you doing??

What is that??

JASMINE. Nothing.

KENDRA. Nothing??

JASMINE. What are you doing home?

Aren't you supposed to be in LA right now?

Don't you have events?

KENDRA. I cancelled them to come back here.

JASMINE. *(Brightening.)* Really?

Why?

KENDRA. Because apparently there have been an alarmingly large number of city-wide blackouts happening here.

JASMINE. ...those blackouts were city-wide?

KENDRA. *City. Wide.*

And no one has been able to explain why.

So I asked myself, what could possibly be causing such a massive power surge that it would repeatedly overload the electrical grid for a city of millions of people.

And after I did a little digging, I was able to track the source of the power surges to one very specific spot... my daughter's bedroom.

JASMINE. Oh...

KENDRA. Yeah.

"Oh."

So my question is

What could my twelve-year-old daughter possibly be doing

That's using more electricity than a small country?

(**KENDRA** *looks pointedly at the time machine.)*

JASMINE. Okay. Promise you won't get mad?

KENDRA. I'm absolutely not going to promise that.

JASMINE. Then I can't tell you.

KENDRA. Jasmine! Yes you will tell me.

JASMINE. No because then I'll be in more trouble than I am right now.

KENDRA. You're gonna be in even more trouble if I have to go ask your dad.

JASMINE. He can't help, he doesn't know anything.

KENDRA. Okay.

(**KENDRA** *starts to go.*)

JASMINE. I solved your theory!

(*Beat.* **KENDRA** *stops.*)

KENDRA. What do you mean you solved my theory?

(**KENDRA** *looks at the machine.*)

(*Then back at her daughter.*)

(*She realizes?*)

(*Re: time machine.*) Is that...?

(**KENDRA** *stares at the time machine in wonder.*)

It works?

JASMINE. Your theory works, Mom.

(**KENDRA** *marvels at it.*)

KENDRA. It works...

(**KENDRA** *realizes something.*)

Wait...have you been *using this*?!

JASMINE. ...Only like a little bit.

KENDRA. Are you kidding me!?!

JASMINE. I'm sorry!

KENDRA. Do you know how unspeakably – how world-endingly dangerous that is?

JASMINE. In our defense, we didn't blow anything up like
I thought we would.

KENDRA. Who's "we"?

(*Beat.*)

JASMINE. Uhhhhhhhh so Uncle Craig might've helped me
a little bit...

KENDRA. Reeeeeally.

JASMINE. It's not his fault! I forced him.

KENDRA. Ohhhhhh wait until I talk to Craig.

JASMINE. Please be easy on him

He's

He's kinda going through a rough time right now.

Mostly because of me...

KENDRA. You are in SO much trouble right now.

JASMINE. I know...

KENDRA. You are *never* allowed to use this machine again,
do you understand me?

JASMINE. I can't...promise that.

KENDRA. Excuse me?

JASMINE. I'm sorry Mom, but I can't promise that.

KENDRA. I'm not giving you a choice here.

JASMINE. I need it.

KENDRA. Why?

JASMINE. Because I want you home!

(*Beat.*)

I want you to be home, Mom.

KENDRA. ...

JASMINE. In your TED Talk, you always talk about this one big regret you have.

This *one thing*

How if you could go back into the past, you'd change it.

And I thought maybe that was you and Dad's divorce.

And if I could just change the past so y'all were together again...

KENDRA. ...Then I'd come home.

Ohhh sweetheart.

JASMINE. But it never worked!

No matter what we did, we could never get y'all back together.

And I think I know why now.

It's because it's not Dad that's the problem, is it?

I think maybe...it's me.

KENDRA. What??

JASMINE. The reason you're never home anymore.

Your regret.

KENDRA. Sweetheart, no.

How could you think that??

JASMINE. Because I'm the only common denominator in all the different realities!

I'm the only thing that never changed.

And I know I'm not the easiest daughter to have.

I know I get into trouble with government agencies sometimes

And the electricity bill is always like so bad.

So maybe if I'm the one that changes, you might want to be home?

KENDRA. No baby girl, I already want to be home!

JASMINE. You only came back today though because you thought I was blowing up the neighborhood.

KENDRA. I came back to make sure you were okay.

JASMINE. But not anything else though…

> *(Beat. This hits* **KENDRA.***)*

KENDRA. You're right.

…

You're right.

I'm so sorry sweetheart.

I should've come back from my tour sooner.

I should've seen what you were going through, but I… I missed it.

I was working so much that I missed it.

…

Sometimes being a parent is like trying to hold the entire world together with just two hands.

Your work

Your child

A divorce

And no matter how hard you try

All you can do is sit there and watch as things slip through your fingers.

And some of those things that slip through?

Those are my great regrets.

JASMINE. What are?

KENDRA. All the days I missed spending with you because I was working.

Every single one that slipped through my fingers.

And wishing there was some way to go back and get them back.

But knowing I couldn't.

And I keep telling myself I'm going to do better.

But then another day passes...and that becomes another regret.

(Slight pause.)

(A realization for **JASMINE.***)*

JASMINE. But...you could actually go back now.

We could go back and change all those days.

All those regrets.

KENDRA. We could...

But anything we change

Even the tiniest bit?

Would end up changing who you are.

And I don't want a different version of who you are.

JASMINE. There might be better versions of me out there though

Ones who don't get into trouble or do things they're not supposed to.

KENDRA. I love that you sometimes get into trouble and do things you're not supposed to.

JASMINE. Even though I took your theory and stole your greatest scientific discovery?

KENDRA. Sweetheart

You are my greatest scientific discovery.

>(**JASMINE** *gets really emotional.*)

JASMINE. You're MY greatest scientific discovery!

>(*They hug for a long time.*)

KENDRA. And you are definitely grounded for a very very very long time.

JASMINE. I know...

>(*Short pause.*)

>(**KENDRA** *sees something in* **JASMINE**'s *hair. She picks at it.*)

(*Swatting her away.*) What are you doing?

KENDRA. You have some fuzz or something, hold on.

JASMINE. Stop, you're gonna mess it up!

KENDRA. Shh, I almost got it.

JASMINE. (*Swatting again.*) Get outta there!

KENDRA. There, I got it, I got it. Okay?

JASMINE. Did you mess it up?

KENDRA. No...

>(*She did. She smooths it down.*)

That's better.

...

I'm sorry I haven't been around as much as I should have baby girl.

JASMINE. I'm sorry too.

For all the blackouts and almost blowing up the house and possibly the solar system.

(They have a moment.)

KENDRA. So wait...how did you go about trying to get me and your dad back together??

JASMINE. We tried to turn him into something more than just a middle school science teacher.

KENDRA. What's wrong with being a middle school science teacher?

They're responsible for the next generation of scientists.

Which in effect...makes them responsible for the future.

And I love that about your dad.

JASMINE. It actually worked once.

KENDRA. Really??

JASMINE. Yeah, but it was weird

He dressed really fancy, it looked strange on him

And he just...he wasn't the same.

(Knock knock.)

*(**DOUG** pops his head in.)*

DOUG. Hey!

What are you doing here?

JASMINE. Dad!

*(**JASMINE** jumps up and hugs her dad.)*

You're back to normal!

DOUG. Was I...different?

KENDRA. Where have you been?

DOUG. I was on a long phone call, I didn't hear you come in.

What's going on?

KENDRA. Oh I don't know

Have you happened to notice any LARGE fluctuations in the electricity

Or presumably any loud loud noises coming from Jasmine's room that might be alarming?

DOUG. Of course.

But there's always huge fluctuations in the electricity and alarming noises coming from her room.

I've got to give her a *little* bit of space, you know?

> (**KENDRA** *sighs. Oh Doug.*)

JASMINE. Are you okay, Dad?

DOUG. Of course popsicle! Why?

JASMINE. You look like you've been crying again.

DOUG. I was definitely *not* crying again.

JASMINE. Dad.

DOUG. I wasn't!

JASMINE. Who were you on the phone with?

> (**DOUG** *sighs real big.*)

> (*Then plops down in a small chair or beanbag.*)

DOUG. Judy.

JASMINE. Ohhhhh, Dad...

DOUG. You were right.

Three weeks.

It's over.

KENDRA. Who's Judy?

JASMINE. The woman who just broke up with Dad.

KENDRA. *(Gasps.)* Is she the woman who you were…

DOUG. Yeah…

I mean it wasn't anything serious, but

I don't know

Kinda felt like it could be something.

KENDRA. That's so brave of you for getting out there though!

I haven't been able to date at all.

I was at a restaurant and some guy tried to get my number and I panicked and ran into the bathroom and didn't leave for half an hour.

DOUG. Isn't it SO scary??

KENDRA. How did you meet this person?

DOUG. *(Ashamed.)* Online…

KENDRA. That is my *nightmare.*

DOUG. It's actually, it's not that bad.

KENDRA. Really??

JASMINE. Wait wait wait you have to check out dad's dating profile.

DOUG. Noooooooooo we / don't need to –

KENDRA. Oh *yes*, please we have to.

JASMINE. Okay okay!

(**JASMINE** *brings up Doug's profile on her computer.*)

KENDRA. Middle Aged Sweethearts, oh Doug…

DOUG. I know, I know…

       (Doug's profile comes up on the screen.)

KENDRA. Oh wow.

Awwww.

Look at your picture.

       (KENDRA *tears up.)*

JASMINE. Yeah, he needs to change his profile picture immediately.

KENDRA. No, I like it.

JASMINE. What?!

KENDRA. It makes you look., I don't know…kind.

It's hard to find "kind" out there.

DOUG. *(Sincerely.)* Thanks.

       (A moment.)

KENDRA. However, let's go down to your three top "interests."

DOUG. What's wrong with my interests?

KENDRA. Doug. Sweetheart. We have got to *talk*.

JASMINE. THANK you.

KENDRA. Can we edit this right now?

JASMINE. I can!

KENDRA. Alright, *first* of all

You cannot list kayaking as an interest if you've never done it.

DOUG. I told you it's

The videos!

I like watching people do it on the YouTube videos.

(The lights slowly dim on **JASMINE** *and her parents as* **KENDRA** *tells* **DOUG** *why his dating profile is so bad.)*

(This scene plays out in the background...)

(...all as a spotlight comes up on a woman who looks very much like **JASMINE** *if she was in her late twenties.)*

(She's about to give a talk.)

(The screen above her reads TED Talk 2038.)

(She looks around the space.)

(Taking in the room.)

FUTURE JASMINE. Many years ago

There was an amazing woman who came up with a theory about how to make all regret in life just... disappear.

All you had to do was push a simple little button

And you would get a do-over to make reality whatever you wanted it to be.

It was a wonderful theory.

However

I have an alternate one.

Which, I believe can be best summed up by this poem a very good friend of mine wrote me when we were twelve.

(She unfolds an old letter.)

It's titled, "Dumped Fourteen Times and Counting."

Oh why oh why

Does she treat me like this plaything

It must be because

I suck at everything

After the first breakup I was sad

After the second I felt broken

But I kept coming back

'Cause my love for you is unbroken

After the sixth time I was hurt

After the seventh I asked why

After the eighth time I was done

And ready to say goodbye

But I keep coming back

For time eleven and twelve and thirteen

Because each time I got stronger

So I could be ready for fourteen

Each time helped me grow

Each time helped me see

You weren't trying to be mean

You just needed to be seen

So I hope that you'll read this

I hope your calls don't end

However, I don't want to go for fifteen

But I'd love to stay friends.

 (The poem is done.)

FUTURE JASMINE. Okay so, real quick, I just want to say that it is wrong to get together with someone and break up with them fourteen times in a row.

You should not do that.

It is, I guess you could say, a regret I have.

But I can't go back and fix it now.

Or rather... I won't.

Because who knows?

Would he and I have the friendship we have today if I went back and erased that?

Would he be the same strong-willed person he is?

Would I be able to understand the value of his friendship?

Would I be able to understand the value of anything I have...?

...

Today, I'd like to offer an alternate theory to my mother's.

That sometimes, scientific progress means *not* fixing our mistakes

And instead...embracing them.

So if you're feeling bad about getting a C minus in school yesterday

Or regret not listening to your parents when they told you not to hack into that major international company

Or feel if you could just go back to last week to change that one thing, everything'd be perfect.

...Let it go.

Because there is no such thing as a perfect reality

There's just *your* reality

And what you choose to make of it.

End of Play

www.ingramcontent.com/pod-product-compliance
Lightning Source LLC
Chambersburg PA
CBHW070327120726
47909CB00008B/2634